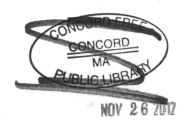

A gift from
the
Lois and Robert Evans, Jr.
Children's Book Fund

Concord Free
Public
Library

On the Road to Mr. MINEO'S

Also by Barbara O'Connor

Beethoven in Paradise

Me and Rupert Goody

Moonpie and Ivy

Fame and Glory in Freedom, Georgia

Taking Care of Moses

How to Steal a Dog

Greetings from Nowhere

The Small Adventure of Popeye and Elvis

The Fantastic Secret of Owen Jester

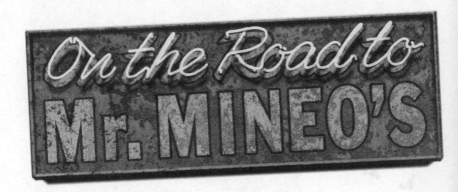

BARBARA O'CONNOR

Frances Foster Books
FARRAR STRAUS GIROUX
New York

Farrar Straus Giroux Books for Young Readers
175 Fifth Avenue, New York 10010

Copyright © 2012 by Barbara O'Connor
Map copyright © 2012 by Greg Call
All rights reserved
Distributed in Canada by D&M Publishers, Inc.
Printed in the United States of America by
RR Donnelley & Sons Company, Harrisonburg, Virginia
First edition, 2012
1 3 5 7 9 10 8 6 4 2

mackids.com

Library of Congress Cataloging-in-Publication Data

O'Connor, Barbara.
    On the road to Mr. Mineo's / Barbara O'Connor. — 1st ed.
        p.   cm.
    Summary: Sherman, a one-legged pigeon, sets everyone aflutter in a
small southern town.
    ISBN 978-0-374-38002-1 (hardcover)
    ISBN 978-0-374-35656-9 (e-book)
    [1. Homing pigeons—Fiction.   2. Pigeons—Fiction.   3. South
Carolina—Fiction.]   I. Title.

PZ7.O217On 2012
[Fic]—dc23

                                                    2011049679

To Frances Foster

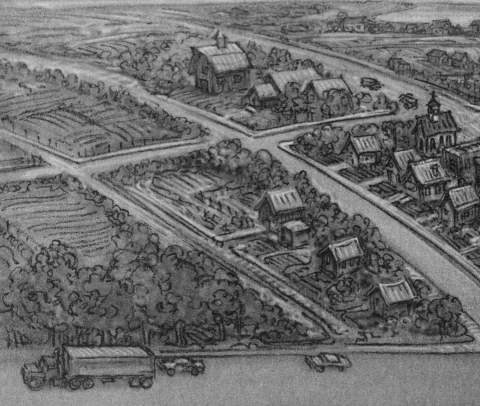

On the Road to Mr. MINEO'S

CHAPTER ONE

Where the Story Begins

Highway 14 stretches on for miles and miles through the South Carolina countryside.

The land is flat.

The dirt is red.

There are mountains to the west. An ocean to the east.

Every few miles there is a gas station. A billboard. A Waffle House.

In the summer, cars whiz up the highway with suitcases strapped on the roofs and bicycles hanging off the backs. Eighteen-wheelers rumble along, hauling lumber and paper and concrete sewer pipes.

The cars and the eighteen-wheelers drive right by a

small green sign with an arrow pointing to the left. The sign reads MEADVILLE.

Pecan trees line the main street of Meadville, shading the sidewalks and dropping pecans for boys to throw at stop signs.

On summer afternoons, waves of steamy heat hover above the asphalt roads.

Tollie Sanborn sits on the curb in front of the barbershop in his white barber coat with combs in the pocket.

Elwin Dayton changes a flat tire on his beat-up car with flames painted on the hood.

Marlene Roseman skips to swimming lessons, her flip-flops slapping on the sidewalk.

When the sun goes down and the moon comes up, the street is empty. The shops are closed and dark. The streetlights flicker on. A stray cat roams the alleys, sniffing at Dumpsters overflowing with rotten lettuce and soggy cardboard boxes.

Just past the post office is a narrow street called Waxhaw Lane. At the end of Waxhaw Lane is a green house with muddy shoes on the porch and an empty doghouse in the front yard.

On one side of the door of the green house is a window. The window is open. The room inside is dark.

A curly-haired girl named Stella sits in the window and whispers into the night:

Moo goo gai pan

Moo goo gai pan

Moo goo gai pan

The words drift through the screen and float across the street and hover under the streetlights, dancing with the moths.

Stella is supposed to be saying her prayers, but instead she is just whispering words, like *moo goo gai pan*.

Across the street from the green house is a big white house with blue-striped awnings over the windows and rocking chairs on the porch. A giant hickory-nut tree casts shadows that move in the warm breeze like fingers wiggling over the dandelions on the dry brown lawn. The roots of the tree lift up patches of cement under the sidewalk out front.

The next morning, Stella will race across the street and up the gravel driveway of the big white house. She will climb the wooden ladder to the flat roof of the garage to wait for Gerald Baxter.

Stella and Gerald will sit in lawn chairs on the roof and play cards on an overturned trash can. They will watch Stella's older brother, Levi, and his friends C.J. and

Jiggs ride their rickety homemade skateboards up and down the street.

They will eat saltine crackers with peanut butter and toss scraps down to Gerald's gray-faced dog sleeping in the ivy below.

They will listen to the kids on Waxhaw Lane playing in somebody's sprinkler or choosing teams for kickball. Stella will want to join them, but Gerald won't. Stella might go anyway, leaving Gerald pouting on the roof. But most likely she will heave a sigh and stay up there on the roof, playing cards with Gerald.

They will watch the lazy days of summer stretch out before them like the highway out by the Waffle House.

As the sun sinks lower in the sky and disappears behind the shiny white steeple of Rocky Creek Baptist Church, the lightning bugs will come out one by one, twinkling across the yards on Waxhaw Lane.

Gerald's mother will turn on the back-porch light, sending a soft yellow glow across the yard. Stella's mother will holler at Levi for leaving his skateboard in the driveway again.

Stella and Gerald will put the cards inside the little shed at the back of the garage roof and climb down the ladder.

The next day will start the same.

Stella will race across the street to the big white house and climb the wooden ladder to the garage roof to wait for Gerald.

But this time something will be different.

CHAPTER TWO

What Stella Saw

Stella raced across the street to the big white house and climbed the wooden ladder to the garage roof to wait for Gerald.

She went back to the shed to get the cards.

She and Gerald had built the shed last summer. It had taken a long time. Searching for scraps of wood in alleys and on the curb on trash day. Hauling the lumber up the ladder to the roof. Figuring out how to fit the pieces together. Sawing. Hammering. Stella having lots of good ideas and Gerald never wanting to try any of them.

But finally they had finished.

The crowning glory of the shed was a roof made of wavy tin they had found in the scrap pile outside Jonas Barkley's house when his flimsy old carport collapsed.

The wavy tin roof was good, but it wasn't perfect. It hung over the edge of the shed and made the door stick. Stella had to yank the door hard to open it. When she did, a startled one-legged bird fluttered wildly on the roof of the shed, its wings flapping and its foot tap, tap, tapping on the tin.

Stella jumped back.

The bird stopped flapping and tapping and looked at her, its head cocked to one side. Its orange eyes blinking.

A pigeon!

Stella had never seen a one-legged pigeon in Meadville, South Carolina.

She had never seen a one-legged pigeon *anywhere*.

"Hey there," she said, not moving a muscle.

The pigeon tucked his leg up under him and sat on the edge of the wavy tin roof.

Stella barely breathed.

She wanted to reach out and stroke the pigeon's smooth, silky back. The gray wings with two black stripes. The iridescent green neck, sparkling like jewels in the morning sun.

"I hate Carlene!" Gerald hollered as he stomped onto the roof, his red hair damp with sweat and stuck to his forehead.

The pigeon flew away in a whirl of flapping feathers and disappeared into the branches of the oak tree above the garage.

"Dang it, Gerald!" Stella slapped her hands against her sides.

Gerald just stood there, looking confused.

"There was a one-legged pigeon on top of the shed." Stella pointed to the wavy tin roof.

Gerald looked up into the tree. "Really?"

"Maybe it'll come back and we can catch it," Stella said.

"Catch it?"

"Yeah."

"What for?"

Stella waved a hand at Gerald. "You never want to do anything fun."

"Yes I do."

Stella rolled her eyes. "You think playing crazy eights the livelong day is fun?" She kicked at the rotten leaves on the garage roof. "Well, I'm sick of it."

"What do you want to do?"

Stella pointed to the branches overhead. "I want to catch that pigeon."

"Okay." Gerald blinked at Stella. His cheeks were fat,

like a chipmunk's, and flushed with the summer heat. "But I still hate Carlene."

Carlene was Gerald's older sister. She painted her fingernails black and argued with a long-haired boy in an old car in her driveway. One time she hollered cuss words at her father right in the middle of the bank.

Stella sort of hated Carlene, too.

"Come on," she said, hurrying down the wooden ladder to the gravel driveway below.

"Where are you going?" Gerald asked worriedly, peering over the edge of the roof.

"To find something to catch that pigeon with." Stella went into the garage, squinting into the darkness, breathing in the smell of dampness and mold and gasoline.

She could hear Gerald clomping down the ladder and then huffing and puffing outside the garage.

"I'm not allowed in there," he called from the doorway.

Stella rummaged through the garden tools, climbed over a rusty lawn mower, and peeked under a torn blue tarp. She stepped over paint cans and greasy car parts. She opened the drawers of a warped and mildewed bureau with missing knobs and poked through the fishing tackle and nails and screwdrivers inside.

"I'm not allowed in there," Gerald called again.

Stella studied all the things hanging on the walls of the garage.

A bicycle wheel. A wooden tennis racket with no strings. A fishing net.

A fishing net?

"Hot dang!" Stella called out, stepping over flowerpots and old tires to get to the net.

"What?" Gerald called.

Stella climbed onto a sawdust-covered workbench.

"What?" Gerald called again.

Stella grabbed the net, hopped off the workbench, stepped over the flowerpots and old tires, and made her way to the door.

"*What?*" Gerald hollered, stomping his foot.

Stella stepped out of the dark garage and into the dappled morning light.

"*This!*" she said, thrusting the fishing net toward him.

Then she wiggled her eyebrows and grinned. "I have a good idea."

CHAPTER THREE

When Gerald Fell Off the Roof

Gerald had a familiar feeling in the pit of his stomach.

Dread.

Whenever Stella got a good idea, something bad almost always happened.

A dent in the side of his father's car.

His grandmother's embroidered tablecloth left out in the rain.

A stripe of black paint that stayed on his forehead for a long time.

And one particularly good idea that eventually involved a fire truck and a crowbar.

The dread in Gerald's stomach worked its way down to his feet, making them heavy, like cinderblocks, as he followed Stella across the driveway.

Crunch

Crunch

Crunch

And even heavier when he climbed the ladder to the garage roof.

Clomp

Clomp

Clomp

By the time he stepped onto the garage roof, the dread was circling around him like a thick, dark cloud.

"Okay," Stella said. "Here's my idea." She pushed at the springy curls that had fallen across her eyes.

"First . . ." She held up one finger. "We look for that pigeon."

"Next . . ." She held up two fingers. "We sit real still so maybe he'll land on the shed again."

"And then . . ." She held up three fingers. "We scoop him up with this net." She waved the net in the air. "Easy peasy," she added.

Gerald shrugged. "Okay," he mumbled.

And so they started step one of Stella's plan.

They looked for the pigeon in the tree branches above the garage.

They looked.

And they looked.

And they looked.

But they didn't see him.

Gerald's cloud of dread started to lift a little.

But then Stella whispered three words that brought it back: "There he is!"

Gerald looked where Stella was pointing into the oak branches overhead. Sure enough, a one-legged pigeon with a shiny green neck was perched above them.

"Shhhh." Stella put her finger to her lips and tiptoed in slow motion over to the lawn chairs. She sat down and patted the seat of the chair beside her. Gerald and his dread sat down.

Then they began step two of Stella's plan. They sat real still so maybe the pigeon would land on the shed again.

They sat.

And they sat.

And they sat.

But the pigeon did not land on the shed again.

And then, just like all the other times that Stella got a good idea, something bad happened.

Stella started spewing out more ideas, and the next

thing Gerald knew he was searching the pantry for pop-corn to toss onto the top of the shed. The pigeon swooped down out of the tree to peck at the popcorn. Stella looked wide-eyed and whispered, "Help me catch him." So Gerald tiptoed around to the other side of the shed, and then he fell off the roof.

CHAPTER FOUR

Why Mr. Mineo Was Aggravated

On the outskirts of town, in a rusty trailer beside a lake, Arthur Mineo scraped meatloaf off a plate and into a dog bowl.

A very fat dog with a stub of a tail waddled out from under the kitchen table and gobbled up the meatloaf.

"Let's go look again, Ernie." Mr. Mineo held the screen door open for the fat dog, and the two of them went around the side of the trailer to a weathered blue shed with a slanting roof. A large wire cage jutted out of one side. The door of the shed was made of chicken wire. The sound of cooing drifted through the door.

The soft cooing of homing pigeons.

Mr. Mineo opened the door and stepped inside. He pointed at the pigeons one by one, calling their names.

Edna

Frankie

Martha

Samson

Leslie

Taylor

Amy

Joe

Christopher

and *Martin*

"Gol-dern it, Ernie," Mr. Mineo called out to the dog. "Where in the heck is Sherman?"

Ernie cocked his head and peered through the door with sad, watery eyes.

"I'm so aggravated." Mr. Mineo stepped out of the shed and searched the sky over the lake.

He walked down to the edge of the water, muttering to Ernie.

"I *knew* that dern fool bird was going to get lost sooner or later.

"I *told* you he was wandering too far from the others.

"I *told* you he was heading off toward Meadville instead of across the lake like he's supposed to.

"He's liable to get into a tussle with a hawk again and lose that other leg.

"Dern fool bird."

Then he trudged back up to the side of the shed and opened a shuttered window. One by one, the pigeons hopped onto the ledge of the window and soared out into the cloudless blue sky.

"Y'all go find Sherman," Mr. Mineo called as they flew off across the lake and disappeared behind the trees on the other side.

While the pigeons flew, Mr. Mineo cleaned the shed.

He swept the floor.

He changed the water bowls.

He scrubbed the perches on the walls.

Mr. Mineo had gotten the homing pigeons from his brother, Carl, who went to live in a nursing home a few months ago. When he had first gotten them, he didn't think he would like them.

But he did.

He didn't think he would enjoy taking care of them.

But he did.

When he was finished cleaning, he scooped birdseed out of a bucket with a coffee can and sprinkled some on the floor. Then he went outside and shook the can, calling, "Come and get it!"

The seed in the can rattled.

Mr. Mineo watched the sky. Before long, a cluster of birds appeared in the distance. When they were over the shed, they circled once or twice. Then they swooped down one by one, landed on top of the wire cage, and hopped through the bars of a small window into the shed.

Edna

Frankie

Martha

Samson

Leslie

Taylor

Amy

Joe

Christopher

and *Martin*

But not Sherman.

Mr. Mineo whistled for Ernie. Then the two of them ambled back up the path to the rusty trailer, Ernie's stub of a tail wagging and Mr. Mineo muttering, "I'm so aggravated."

CHAPTER FIVE

Gerald Gets Stuck in the Shrubbery

One minute Gerald was there.

And the next minute he wasn't.

Stella peered over the edge of the roof. Gerald had lucked out. He had landed in the thick shrubbery along the side of the garage.

"You lucked out!" she called down to Gerald.

From somewhere in the distance came the tinkling music of an ice cream truck. Stella fought the urge to hurry down the ladder and go look for it. She peered down at Gerald, sprawled on his back in the shrubbery.

He looked a little surprised, his eyes wide and his mouth opened in an O shape.

"You okay?" she called to him.

Gerald blinked up at her. "I can't move," he whispered.

"Why not?"

Gerald started to cry.

"Stay right there." Stella scrambled down the ladder and ran around to the side of the garage.

"Whatever you do," she said, "don't cry."

Stella's brother, Levi, had a nose for crying kids. He sniffed them out like a coonhound. Then he and his scabby-kneed, germ-infested friends C.J. and Jiggs would laugh and taunt and joke and poke and generally make life more miserable for whoever was crying.

Especially Gerald.

"I can't move," Gerald whispered again, sniffling.

"Are you paralyzed?" Stella poked at Gerald's chubby white knee.

"Prickers," he said in a quivering voice.

"What?"

"Prickers."

Sure enough, the shrubbery that Gerald had had the good luck to land in was filled with prickers. Sharp, mean-looking prickers that grabbed at Gerald's shirt and left angry red scratches on his arms and legs.

"What am I going to do?" Gerald looked at Stella out of the corner of his eye, keeping his head still, his neck stiff.

Stella tapped her chin. "Hmmm," she said. "Let me think."

Stella thought.

And Gerald waited.

Stella thought.

And Gerald waited.

"Okay," she said. "I have a good idea."

Gerald groaned.

"We'll hold hands," she said. "And then, on the count of three, I'll pull you out." She beamed at Gerald. "Trust me," she added. "I'll do it so fast you won't feel a thing."

Gerald looked at Stella in a wild-eyed kind of way and said, "But I don't want to."

Stella jammed her fists into her waist. "You want Levi and those germ-infested friends of his to get a whiff of you stuck in the bushes crying?"

Gerald's eyes grew wider.

"Okay, then," Stella said. "Let's do it."

She took both of Gerald's hands in hers.

"On the count of three," she said.

"One.

"Two.

"Three."

Stella tugged.

And tugged.

And tugged some more.

It took a lot more tugs than Stella thought it would. She tried to ignore Gerald's hollering and just concentrate on tugging.

Finally, Gerald was free. He lay on the ground beside the shrubbery in a scratched-up, torn-shirt heap. Stella stood over him, her hands on her knees.

His eyes were closed.

"Gerald?"

He opened one eye.

And then the other one.

"Okay, good," Stella said. Then she raced over to the garage and started up the ladder to look for the one-legged pigeon.

CHAPTER SIX

Gerald Finally Says No

Gerald blinked up at the sky.

He took a breath in.

He let a breath out.

He was still alive. But he was all scratched up and ached from head to toe.

Stella poked her head over the edge of the garage roof and whispered, "That pigeon's back." Her curly hair stood out around her head like a lion's mane.

"Leave me alone," Gerald said, examining his scratched-up arms.

"I have another idea," Stella whispered down to him.

Gerald sighed.

"We'll make a trap," she said.

Gerald picked leaves out of his hair, pretending like he didn't hear her.

"We can use the trash can and prop it up with a stick and tie a string to the stick and put some birdseed under it and . . ."

Gerald limped over to the back porch. He dabbed at his arms and legs with his shirttail while Stella yammered away about her cockamamie idea. He wanted her to go home.

Stella came down the ladder and disappeared into the garage.

Gerald pretended not to notice.

A few minutes later, she came out of the garage with a long wooden dowel and skipped over to the ladder. "Come on," she called as she scrambled back up to the roof.

Gerald heaved another sigh.

Then he plodded, stoop-shouldered, to the ladder and climbed up to the roof to join Stella.

***

They spent all afternoon working on the trap that Stella had designed. But they had a lot of problems.

The trash can wouldn't stay propped up with the dowel.

The dowel was too long.

The trash can was too big.

Then Stella tried to convince Gerald to climb over the fence to the yard next door and borrow a little birdseed from Mildred Perry's bird feeder.

"Come on, Gerald," Stella said. "Please?"

"No."

"Why not?"

"Because."

"Give me one good reason."

Gerald gave Stella three good reasons:

1. Mildred Perry had a big mangy dog that once ate his sister's purse.
2. Mildred Perry had a teenage son who smoked cigarettes and squealed the tires of his pickup truck in the middle of the night.
3. He didn't want to.

Stella looked a little surprised.

Gerald *felt* a little surprised. He never said no to Stella.

She plopped down on one of the lawn chairs and crossed her arms, glaring at him.

The sun was beginning to sink behind the trees. Lightning bugs flickered down in the yard below. Gerald's gray-faced dog whined at the back door.

And high above the rooftops of Meadville, a one-legged pigeon headed toward the outskirts of town.

CHAPTER SEVEN

Little Brown Dog

On the far end of Main Street, where the shops ended and the cornfields and orchards began, was a farm with a small brick house and a big wooden barn. A little brown dog had been living in the big wooden barn.

Nobody fed the little brown dog.

Nobody played with the little brown dog.

Nobody loved the little brown dog.

Amos and Ethel Roper lived in the brick house and had no idea the little brown dog was living in the barn.

Amos and Ethel had no children to take care of. Theirs were all grown up and had flown the coop, as Amos often said.

"You spend half your life wiping their noses and

buying them stuff they don't need and driving them to the emergency room for stitches and then they fly the coop," he complained.

Amos and Ethel had no crops to take care of. The big fancy cannery down in Columbia had bought the Ropers' fields and sent big fancy machines to harvest the beans and the corn.

So Amos and Ethel had a lot of time to argue.

They argued about whether to fix that rotten railing on the back porch or just let the dang thing fall off.

They argued about whether to cut down the sweet gum tree that was shading their small tomato garden under the kitchen window or to move the tomatoes out by the clothesline.

And they argued about what kind of critter had been hanging around the place at night.

Something had been getting into the garbage by the back door.

Something had been scratching at the soft, rotting wood of the barn.

And *something* had been making holes in the dry red dirt under the old pig trough.

Amos was convinced it was a raccoon.

Ethel was convinced it was a skunk.

They argued and argued.

But when they were awakened in the middle of the night by the sharp, frantic barking of a dog out in the barn, they knew they had both been wrong.

"A dog!" Ethel said, padding to the window in her bare feet and her thin flowered nightgown.

"I told you it wasn't a skunk," Amos said, pulling the sheet over his head.

The dog barked and barked and barked some more.

"What are we going to do?" Ethel said.

Zzzzzz.

Amos's snores swirled around the room and irritated Ethel. She took a flashlight out of the drawer of the night-stand and went to the back door.

The dog was still barking. She shined the flashlight across the yard. Everything seemed so still and spooky.

The clothesline.

The wheelbarrow.

The broken lawn mower.

The hose snaking from the faucet over to the tomato patch.

Ethel crept down the back steps and out into the yard. The tall grass was cool and damp beneath her bare feet.

When she got closer to the barn and shined the flashlight in big sweeping arcs, the dog stopped barking.

Ethel shivered in the breezy night air. She should have grabbed her sweater from the coat rack by the back door. She tiptoed over the smooth, packed dirt of the path that led to the barn.

The dog barked again. One uncertain yip of a bark.

Ethel shined the flashlight into the half-open door of the barn.

There was a very faint rustle in the pile of old hay in the corner.

There was a very faint fluttering of wings up in the rafters.

There was a very faint pitter-patter of Ethel's heart under her thin flowered nightgown.

She shined the flashlight into the corner where she had heard the faint rustle. A little brown dog stood knee-deep in the hay, looking up into the rafters.

Ethel shined the flashlight into the hayloft above her. A pigeon sat nestled in a deserted barn-owl nest where the rafter met the roof.

"Who invited y'all into my barn?" Ethel called, stepping through the door.

The pigeon flapped and fluttered in the rafters

overhead, then landed on the rotting floor of the hayloft and hopped frantically on one leg before swooping out of the large opening near the top of the barn roof.

The little brown dog dashed across the barn past Ethel, nearly knocking her off her feet as he scrambled out the door and disappeared into the darkness.

The faint pitter-patter of Ethel's heart turned into a *ba-boom, ba-boom, ba-boom.* She staggered backward, tripped over that ancient milk bucket she had told Amos to move about a million times, dropped the flashlight, and landed with an *oomph* on the dusty barn floor.

And while all the rustling and fluttering and dashing and swooping and oomphing was going on out in the barn, a loud, steady *zzzzz* drifted out of the Ropers' bedroom window, swirled over the path to the barn, and irritated Ethel.

CHAPTER EIGHT

Pigeon in the Moonlight

Fee fi fo fum
Fee fi fo fum
Fee fi fo fum

Stella whispered words through her bedroom window.

The words swirled around in the still night air and danced dreamily up Waxhaw Lane.

Across the street, in the big white house with blue-striped awnings, Gerald stared at the ceiling and worried.

He had never said no to Stella before.

He tiptoed to his window and peered out into the darkness. Somewhere in the distance a cat was yowling. The mournful sound echoed up the empty Main Street of Meadville.

While Stella whispered and Gerald worried and the

cat yowled, a little brown dog trotted along the side of the road.

And high above the fields and road signs and telephone poles on the outskirts of town, a one-legged pigeon flew silently in the moonlight.

CHAPTER NINE

The Boy Who Cried Wolf

Just beyond the Ropers' small brick house, there was a long dirt driveway. At the end of the driveway was a cluster of ramshackle houses. Living in each of the ramshackle houses was a family named Raynard.

Earl and Maude Raynard and their tiny baby, Earl Jr.

Jackson and Yolanda Raynard and their five kids, whose names all started with the letter *B*.

Emmaline Raynard and her three dogs and four cats and a ferret that smelled bad all the time.

And Alvin and Celia Raynard and their son, whose real name was Lawson but whom everyone called Mutt.

Mutt Raynard was a liar.

Everyone knew it.

Mutt lied about almost everything.

What he ate for breakfast.

Where he caught the catfish he brought home for dinner.

How he lost his shoes.

Almost everything.

Maude Raynard called him the Boy Who Cried Wolf. "Look, Mutt," she told him. "Nobody's ever gonna believe one dang thing you say, even when you tell the truth. Like the Boy Who Cried Wolf."

But that didn't seem to have much of an impact on Mutt.

Sometimes he told the truth.

And sometimes he lied.

And nobody knew which was which and nobody really cared anymore.

So when Mutt told everyone that a one-legged pigeon had landed on his head, nobody paid any attention.

The next day, when he told them it had happened again, nobody paid any attention.

"I *swear*," he said. "A one-legged pigeon. He came swooping out of nowhere and landed right on my head." He patted the top of his head. "Up yonder by the lake." He threw his skinny arm out in the direction of the lake.

But nobody paid any attention.

So Mutt was going to go to the lake every day and wait for that pigeon to show up again. And when it did, he would catch it. He would put it in a cardboard box and take it to each of the Raynard houses and say, "See? I *told* you a one-legged pigeon landed on my head."

CHAPTER TEN

Levi and His Scabby-Kneed, Germ-Infested Friends

As waves of steamy heat hovered above the asphalt on Waxhaw Lane, three boys sat in the shade of a carport, complaining.

It was too hot.

There was nothing to do.

They were hungry.

They were thirsty.

And one of them had poison ivy.

They wished they were at the lake.

They wished they were in the mountains.

They wished they were anywhere but under a carport in Meadville, South Carolina.

When they couldn't think of anything else to complain

about, they took turns flipping bottle caps into the middle of an old tire.

The morning plodded along.

Minute after boring minute.

Across the street a sprinkler sputtered in circles in Gerald Baxter's yard, while his gray-faced dog snored in the sun on the sidewalk out front.

Somewhere up the street, kids were hollering "Not it!"

And then something strange happened.

A one-legged pigeon landed right beside the old tire under the carport.

The boys stared in disbelief.

One of the boys, Levi, whispered, "I'm going to catch him."

The other two boys, C.J. and Jiggs, nodded.

Levi lunged for the pigeon. There was a swirl of flapping wings, and Levi landed on his stomach with a thud as the pigeon flew off, disappearing over the top of the Baxters' house.

Levi scrambled to his feet and called, "Come on!" as he raced across the street, with C.J. and Jiggs hurrying after him.

CHAPTER ELEVEN

Diddly-Squat

Stella and Gerald sat in the lawn chairs on the garage roof and ate waffles in silence, dipping them into syrup in a paper cup.

Stella had tried to stay mad at Gerald for not helping her with the pigeon trap.

That morning, instead of racing across the street and climbing the wooden ladder to the garage roof, she had sat inside the empty doghouse in her front yard and made a beaded necklace.

She wrote swear words with a stick in the dirt at the edge of the road and then rubbed them out with the toe of her sandal.

She made a jump rope out of clothesline and hopped

on her right foot up the sidewalk and on her left foot down the sidewalk.

But then she got bored.

So she had sauntered across the street and climbed the wooden ladder to the garage roof. Gerald had been sitting there, eating waffles and looking forlorn.

He had offered her a waffle.

So here they sat, dipping and eating.

Dipping and eating.

And then something very unexpected happened.

The one-legged pigeon appeared out of nowhere, swooped down, and landed on Gerald's shoulder.

Stella couldn't believe her eyes.

"Be still," she whispered.

The pigeon bobbed his head in that funny way that pigeons bob their heads.

Gerald sat in gape-mouthed shock.

The pigeon made a little cooing sound.

Stella loved his orange eyes. His sparkling green neck. His smooth gray feathers with two black stripes.

"I'm going to pick him up," she whispered. She reached out slowly and lifted the pigeon off of Gerald's shoulder.

Stella had never held a pigeon before.

She could feel his little pigeon heart beating against her fingers.

"What are you going to do with him?" Gerald asked.

"Keep him."

"Keep him?"

Stella clutched the pigeon gently against her chest and stroked his soft back with her finger. "Everybody has a pet but me," she said.

"But you want a dog," Gerald said.

"I used to want a dog." Stella kissed the pigeon on the top of his head. "Now I want a pigeon."

"But where are you going to keep him?" Gerald said.

Stella rolled her eyes. Gerald was so annoying sometimes.

"Right here." She glanced around her at the shed and the chairs and the overturned trash can.

"Here?"

"Why not?"

If Stella had needed the perfect word to describe Gerald's expression, the word would most definitely have been *skeptical*.

"What're y'all doing?" Levi poked his head up over the edge of the roof.

The pigeon fluttered wildly in Stella's hands and she let go. It flew up into the branches overhead.

"Dang it, Levi," Stella hollered.

Levi stepped onto the roof of the garage, followed by C.J. and Jiggs.

"Y'all can't come up here," Stella said, stomping her foot.

Levi was not allowed on the roof of Gerald's garage. Gerald's father had showed up at Stella and Levi's house one day last fall and told their mother about Levi throwing acorns off the roof and leaving little dents in the aluminum siding on the back of their house.

Levi was not even allowed in Gerald's *yard*. Gerald's mother had seen him spitting in the camellias.

"You had that one-legged pigeon," Levi said.

Stella glanced at Gerald, who slumped over in the lawn chair and stared at his sneakers.

"I did not," Stella said.

"I just saw him," Levi said.

"You did not!"

"I did too!"

The next few minutes were a blur of hollering and cussing and kicking and hitting.

When Levi hit Stella on the arm with his famous

Knuckle of Death, she let out a yelp. But she was *not* going to cry.

She turned to Gerald. "Tell them to get off your garage," she said.

Gerald didn't say a word. His face was pale. His chin quivered.

"Go away," Stella hollered at Levi, shoving him with both hands. Maybe he would fall off the roof and land in the prickery shrubbery below.

Levi pushed her back, and there was another whirl of hollering and punching, with C.J. and Jiggs cheering them on and Gerald watching in wild-eyed terror.

"You're not *allowed* up here," Stella yelled at Levi.

"He's *my* pigeon." Levi pointed up into the branches.

"He is not."

"He is too."

"He's *my* pigeon," Stella said. "I found him and I'm keeping him."

"I found him first," Levi said.

"You did not."

"I did so," Levi said. "You can't keep a pigeon, ninny-brain. You don't know diddly-squat about pigeons."

"Yes I do." Stella kicked at a pile of dried oak leaves.

"Name one thing you know about pigeons." Levi and C.J. and Jiggs poked each other and snickered.

Stella scrambled to think of something she knew about pigeons. She was sure she *must* know diddly-squat. She might even know *more* than diddly-squat. But before she could come up with something, the pigeon fluttered off the branch and disappeared over the rooftops of Waxhaw Lane.

"Now look what you did," Stella said.

"Finders keepers, losers weepers," Levi said.

"What do you mean?"

"Whoever finds that pigeon first gets to keep him."

Stella could feel her face burning and her chin quivering.

Don't cry.

Don't cry.

Don't cry, she told herself.

And then, thank the good Lord, just as the tears started, Gerald's mother banged on the side of the garage with a broom and hollered, "You boys get down off of there and go on home!"

CHAPTER TWELVE

Little Brown Dog

Amos wanted to lock the barn door at night and nail plywood over the opening up near the rafters.

But Ethel had a hissy fit.

"That little dog isn't hurting anybody," she told Amos.

"What's wrong with a dog sleeping in the barn?" she asked him.

"And worrying about a one-legged pigeon," Ethel snapped. "For heaven's sake, Amos, what's gotten into you?"

When Amos complained that the dog's barking kept him up at night, she snapped, "If that dog is keeping you up at night, then who in the name of Bessie is that old geezer snoring in my bed?"

Amos flapped his hand at her and ambled out to his chair in the shade by the tomato garden.

Ethel puttered around the kitchen. Every now and then she glanced out the window at Amos. Finally, she saw his eyes close and his head droop until his whiskery chin rested on his chest.

When she heard his soft snoring, she opened the cupboard under the sink, pushed aside the dish detergent and spray cleaner and sponges, and pulled out a small bag of dog food.

She shook some into a pie tin. Then she tossed in a piece of sausage from breakfast, a scoop of tuna from lunch, and a slice of bread. She put the bag of dog food back up under the sink and went out into the yard. She held the pie tin behind her back and tiptoed past Amos, who was still snoring beside the garden. Then she hurried out to the barn and set the pie tin on the floor beneath the ladder to the hayloft.

CHAPTER THIRTEEN

That Dern Fool Bird

Mr. Mineo frowned as he drove his truck up the narrow road to his bait shop. His fat dog, Ernie, sat beside him with his head out the window, ears flapping in the breeze. Rakes and shovels and tire irons and fishing poles clanged and rattled in the back of the truck. A metal toolbox slid from one side to the other.

"Holler if you see him," Mr. Mineo said to Ernie.

When they pulled into the gravel parking lot of the bait shop, the truck bounced and squeaked and groaned before it came to a stop, sending a swirl of dust into the still summer air.

Mr. Mineo got out and searched the sky overhead. Then he shuffled across the parking lot in his scuffed-up brown shoes with Ernie waddling along behind him.

The bait shop was made of cinderblocks and mismatched wood and big squares of dented rusty tin. A warped piece of plywood leaned against the front. Worms for Sale was painted on the plywood in squiggly black letters.

Mr. Mineo unlocked the door of the shop and stepped inside. He turned on the old fan on top of the soda cooler. It hummed and whirred and rattled, blowing paper napkins and candy wrappers around the dark, cluttered room.

"Now where did I put that birdseed?" Mr. Mineo said, pushing aside cardboard boxes and stacks of old fishing magazines.

Ernie plopped down with a groan onto his worn, dirty rug by the door.

"Aha!" Mr. Mineo took the top off a plastic bucket and scooped out birdseed with an empty pork-and-beans can. Then he went outside to the parking lot and rattled the can.

"Come and get it!" he called.

He scanned the sky over the bait shop.

He peered onto the roof.

He looked up into the branches of the trees beside the shop.

"I'm so aggravated," he mumbled to himself.

He went back inside the bait shop and put a big black *X* over the day on the calendar.

Now there were four *X*s.

Sherman had been gone for four days.

Mr. Mineo nudged his dog with the toe of his scuffed brown shoe. "Come on, Ernie," he said.

Then he went back outside and sat on the bench in front of the bait shop and watched the sky, muttering, "That dern fool bird."

CHAPTER FOURTEEN

Stella Does a Very Un-Stella-Like Thing

Gerald knew he should have been embarrassed when his mother hollered at Levi and his scabby-kneed, germ-infested friends. But instead he was relieved.

He tried not to smile as he watched the boys mumbling and grumbling and stomping up Waxhaw Lane toward town.

Then Gerald got the shock of his life when he turned around and saw that Stella was crying.

Stella never cried.

Gerald felt a little embarrassed.

"Um," he said.

Stella wiped her nose with the palm of her hand.

"Um," he said again.

Stella sat with her chin on her knees, sniffling.

Gerald had felt the pain of Levi's Knuckle of Death and cried every time.

But Stella never did.

"Why are you crying?" he asked.

"I want that pigeon," Stella said glumly.

Gerald sat next to her and stared at his shoes.

"Levi always ruins everything," she said.

Gerald couldn't argue with that.

"He's so mean."

Gerald couldn't argue with that, either.

Then Stella did a very un-Stella-like thing.

She knelt in front of him, put her hands together like she was praying, and said in a soft, un-Stella-like voice, "Will you help me catch that pigeon?"

Gerald blinked. "Um . . ."

"Please?"

Say no, Gerald told himself.

Say no, he told himself again.

"Okay," he mumbled.

Stella jumped up and let out a whoop.

Then she dashed to the ladder and hurried down, leaving Gerald sitting on the roof, wishing like anything he had said no.

CHAPTER FIFTEEN

Luther's Chinese Takeout

On the main street of Meadville, two men played checkers on a plastic milk crate in front of Luther's Chinese Takeout.

One of them was pale and thin with a fire-breathing dragon tattooed on one arm, the flames shooting all the way down to the back of his hand.

That was Luther.

The other one had a shiny bald head and a fat round stomach that hung over his belt buckle.

That was Edsel.

Luther and Edsel played checkers nearly every day when Edsel drove down from Rock Hill to deliver produce to Luther's Chinese Takeout.

Luther was not very good at playing checkers.

"Pay up," Edsel would say, flapping his palm out toward Luther.

Edsel always climbed back into his white delivery van with Luther's wrinkled dollar bill in his pocket.

He didn't feel bad about taking Luther's money because the next time he came to Meadville, he would bring Luther a case of that root beer he liked or a bag of warm boiled peanuts or a couple of bass he'd caught down at the lake.

Sometimes, a perky curly-haired girl and a solemn red-headed boy stopped by to watch them play checkers.

Stella and Gerald.

Every now and then, they had some burning question to ask, like how to use a ratchet wrench or where to find a compass.

Sometimes Gerald sat on the hot sidewalk, his freckled legs crossed, his face serious, watching the checker game. Stella would grow bored after about a minute and tug at Gerald's shirt, urging him on to something more interesting.

But today Stella and Gerald raced right past Luther and Edsel without stopping.

Across the street, three boys rode skateboards up and down the sidewalk.

Levi, C.J., and Jiggs.

Every now and then one of them would holler a cuss word or spit into the street.

"Troublemakers," Edsel muttered.

As the afternoon wore on, Edsel beat Luther at checkers three times. Tollie Sanborn came out of the barbershop to turn the crank that closed the awning over the window. Marlene Roseman marched home from dancing lessons in her tap shoes, twirling an invisible baton.

Finally, Luther stretched and yawned and swept the checkers into a shoebox. He folded up the checkerboard and handed Edsel a dollar bill. "Looks like rain."

Edsel glanced at the graying sky and nodded.

Suddenly, a ruckus started across the street.

Stella and Gerald and those three troublemakers on skateboards were in the alley between the bank and the post office. There was a lot of yelling and name-calling, and then the three troublemakers took off up the sidewalk while Stella hurled gravel at them.

Edsel shook his head and asked Luther what the world was coming to.

Luther shrugged.

Then Stella ran across the street toward them with Gerald following, solemn-faced as ever.

"Have y'all seen a one-legged pigeon?" Stella asked.

Edsel made a grumpy face and said, "No."

Luther scratched his chin and shook his head. "Nope."

Then Stella raced off up the sidewalk toward Waxhaw Lane with Gerald hurrying after her.

Edsel made a *hmmph* sound and climbed into his white delivery van.

Luther waved goodbye and went inside his restaurant to make egg rolls.

Overhead, the clouds began to darken. There was a faint, low rumble of thunder. Raindrops began to fall, one by one, onto the streets of Meadville.

Plunk

Plunk

Plunk

And as Edsel's delivery van headed up Highway 14, a one-legged pigeon flew through the summer rain toward a big wooden barn on the outskirts of town.

CHAPTER SIXTEEN

Little Brown Dog

Amos and Ethel Roper had argued all day long.

Amos thought Ethel shouldn't feed the little brown dog in the barn.

Ethel thought that if she fed the little brown dog, he wouldn't get in the garbage at night.

Amos said the last thing they needed was a mangy old stray hanging around.

Ethel said that maybe the dog would scare away the mice that had been chewing the wiring on the tractor.

Amos said he never used that old tractor anyway.

Argue.

Argue.

Argue.

All day long.

That evening, they sat on the back porch. The rain had finally stopped and the dark clouds were beginning to drift away.

Ethel loved this time of day. The time between supper and bedtime, when the harsh shadows in the yard softened and everything seemed a little slower. The birds on the fence post out front. The butterflies on the wildflowers along the driveway.

She loved how the morning glories on the vine that wrapped around the clothesline closed up. How the buzz of the bees in the garden gave way to the croak of bullfrogs down in the pond.

Ethel commented to Amos that the mailman had been awfully late that morning. She mentioned that the strawberries she had bought at the farmers' market were way overpriced. She pointed out how that flower box under the kitchen window was starting to tilt to one side.

But Amos didn't answer.

His head was nodding.

His cheeks were puffing out with each breath.

"Come on, Amos," Ethel said. "Let's go to bed."

But later that night, they woke to the sound of barking again.

Amos made some grumpy, grumbling noises and flipped and flopped in the bed.

Ethel got up and looked out the window. The moon cast a glow over the backyard. The rain had left little puddles in the dirt under the clothesline.

A bird flew around the top of the barn, swooping and gliding in the moon glow.

Out by the old pig trough, the dog barked.

Ethel slipped her favorite sweater over her nightgown, plopped Amos's old straw hat over her thin gray hair, and grabbed the flashlight on the nightstand. She padded into the kitchen, put on her muddy garden shoes, and tucked a graham cracker into the pocket of her sweater. She flipped on the back-porch light and went outside.

The clothesline cast an eerie shadow across the yard, like a long black snake that slithered through the tomato garden, over the woodpile, and across the lawn chair where Amos napped in the afternoon.

As Ethel crossed the yard, the bird swooped through the opening near the roof of the barn and disappeared inside. The dog ran barking after it.

Ethel shined the flashlight through the barn door. The dog stopped barking.

Ethel stepped inside. It smelled like hay and motor oil and something rotten. She shined the flashlight into the corner of the barn.

She had never seen a more pitiful sight.

The little brown dog, wet and shivering.

"Why you wanna bark like that and wake everybody up?" Ethel said to the dog.

He cocked his head and backed up a step or two. She tossed the graham cracker onto the floor. He darted over and gobbled it up.

Ethel shined the flashlight into the rafters.

The one-legged pigeon hopped from one side of the rafter to the other, cooing softly. Then he hopped into the old barn owl's nest, blinking down at Ethel in the glow of the flashlight.

When Ethel turned back to the dog, she was surprised to see that he was sleeping, all curled up in a pile of wet hay in the corner of the barn.

So she picked up the empty pie tin beneath the ladder to the hayloft and went back to the house to fill it with cold spaghetti left over from dinner.

CHAPTER SEVENTEEN

The Boy Who Cried Wolf

Mutt Raynard jumped off the front porch onto the rain-soaked grass. The sun was just peeking over the top of Emmaline Raynard's house. The morning air smelled fresh and clean.

He hopped over the puddles in the dirt driveway.

The sound of Earl Jr.'s crying drifted out of Earl and Maude Raynard's windows.

Jackson and Yolanda Raynard's kids, whose names all started with the letter *B*, were yelling in the backyard.

Mutt headed toward the narrow road to the lake.

He used to walk right up the middle of that road just because he could. There were almost never any cars. Once in a while somebody drove up to the bait shop, but not very often. Then one time his father had driven up behind him in his truck. He had slammed on the brakes, jumped out of the truck, yanked Mutt by the collar, and hollered, "Don't you *never* walk in the middle of the road no more. You hear me?"

So Mutt almost never did.

As he got closer to the lake, he looked up into the morning sky.

No pigeon.

When he turned down the path that led to his favorite fishing spot, way back in a secluded cove, he looked up again.

No pigeon.

He sat on a rock by the edge of the lake and waited.

No pigeon.

Before long, he got bored. He should have brought his fishing rod.

The sun climbed higher in the sky. A dragonfly flitted around in front of him and landed on the rock. He tossed a pebble into the lake. It landed with a *ploink* that made the dragonfly dart away.

And then . . .

. . . a one-legged pigeon landed on his head.

Mutt grabbed for the pigeon with both hands.

But the pigeon flapped his wings wildly and soared off into the morning sky, disappearing over the treetops.

Mutt stomped his feet.

Dang.

Dang.

Dang.

He was more determined than ever to catch that pigeon.

And when he did, everyone would see that he *had* been telling the truth.

CHAPTER EIGHTEEN

Morning on Main Street

Luther helped Edsel unload the produce from his white delivery van.

Lettuce.

Onions.

Celery.

Then they set up the checker game on top of the milk crate and began to play. Every now and then rainwater dripped from the awning overhead onto the checkerboard.

They didn't even look up when Tollie Sanborn unlocked the door of the barbershop across the street and went inside.

Old Mrs. Banner, who worked at the bank, parked her

shiny Cadillac in her usual spot and clomped past Luther and Edsel in her thick-soled shoes.

She nodded to them as she passed, her mouth set in a thin, sharp line.

Luther and Edsel nodded back.

When she disappeared inside the bank, Edsel muttered, "Battle-ax," his eyes still on the checkerboard.

Luther chuckled.

One by one, the residents of Meadville came out onto the rain-soaked sidewalks of Main Street to start their days while Luther and Edsel concentrated on their checker game.

Jolene Hawkins carried an overflowing basket of clothes into the Laundromat.

Dwight Malcolm hung the flag out in front of the post office.

Bitsy Patterson hollered "Hurry up!" to her two runny-nosed children as she hurried into the pharmacy.

Cars drove by and windows opened and cats stretched in the morning sun.

Children rode their bikes through puddles along the edge of the street, sending sprays of dirty water onto the sidewalks.

But Luther and Edsel didn't pay much attention to anything except their game.

In fact, they didn't even notice when a little brown dog trotted right past them and turned up the alley, while a one-legged pigeon sat on the rain-soaked awning above them.

CHAPTER NINETEEN

Stella Smells a Rat

Stella rode her bike up and down the streets of Meadville, searching for the one-legged pigeon. Gerald rode along behind her.

"Are you looking?" she kept calling back to him.

"Yes," he kept saying.

But Stella could tell he wasn't.

Suddenly, Stella stopped. "Shhhh," she said to Gerald. She ducked behind the pecan tree in front of the pharmacy and pointed. Gerald wiped his forehead with his shirttail, exposing his flabby white stomach, and looked in the direction she was pointing.

Levi and C.J. and Jiggs were gathered on the sidewalk in front of the post office.

There was someone with them.

Stella squinted.

Mutt Raynard!

What was *he* doing here?

He almost never came into town.

He stayed out there with all those wild Raynard kids who lived in the cluster of ramshackle houses.

Stella glared up the sidewalk at Levi and the others. "I smell a rat," she said.

"How come?" Gerald scratched at his splotchy red neck.

"That's Mutt Raynard."

"I hate him," Gerald said.

"I bet you anything they're talking about that pigeon," Stella said. "I bet Levi is asking Mutt to help him. Mutt'll do anything. He's crazy."

"Yeah," Gerald said. "He's crazy."

Stella shook her head. "I smell a rat."

CHAPTER TWENTY

The Lie That Levi Loved

Gerald Baxter eats dirt. He crawls up under the hydrangea bushes with a spoon in his back pocket. He hunkers down against the cool, moss-covered bricks of his house and scrapes and scrapes at the dry dirt.

He puts the dirt into his mouth and chews and chews.

"No way!" Levi said when Mutt told him that glorious lie.

Levi loved a good lie, and Mutt told the best ones in Meadville.

"So that means Gerald Baxter has worms," Levi said, "because eating dirt gives you worms."

C.J. and Jiggs hooted and hollered and slapped their scabby knees, laughing up a storm.

Then Levi told Mutt about the one-legged pigeon.

Mutt raised his eyebrows.

"And we've got to catch that thing before Stella and Wormy do," Levi said.

C.J. and Jiggs hooted and hollered again.

"So if you see it," Levi went on, "catch it and bring it to us, okay?"

"I saw that pigeon," Mutt said.

"Really?"

Mutt nodded.

"Where?"

"Up yonder by the Laundromat."

Levi narrowed his eyes at Mutt. "You lying?"

Mutt shrugged. "Maybe it wasn't the same pigeon you're looking for." He picked at dirt under his fingernails. "There's probably lots of one-legged pigeons around here."

Levi glanced up toward the Laundromat.

Mutt shrugged again. "Shiny green head. Black stripes on his wings."

"Come on, y'all," Levi called to C.J. and Jiggs as he took off running toward the Laundromat.

Then Mutt trotted up the sidewalk toward Luther's Chinese Takeout, searching for the one-legged pigeon.

CHAPTER TWENTY-ONE

Amy and That Temper of Hers

Ernie rested his head on Mr. Mineo's scuffed-up brown shoes while Mr. Mineo ate cold macaroni and cheese and rambled on and on about Sherman.

"He's never been gone this long before," he said, tossing a piece of macaroni onto the linoleum floor for Ernie.

"Amy's gonna be ticked off big-time," he said. "Her out in that shed day and night, waiting on him to come home and him off gallivanting all over tarnation and back."

He pushed himself up out of his old plaid lounge chair and shuffled to the kitchen.

"When he does show hisself back in that shed, she's liable to peck him bald-headed," he said. "You know Amy and that temper of hers."

He put the dirty bowl in the sink with the others and called to Ernie, "Let's go see if he's back yet."

They went around the side of the trailer to the shed. The rain had turned the red dirt on the path into gooey red mud. Inside the shed, some of the pigeons pranced around in the chicken-wire cage on the side. Some of them pecked at grains of gritty dirt on the floor. And others sat contentedly on perches.

Mr. Mineo said hello to each one.

Edna

Frankie

Martha

Samson

Leslie

Taylor

Amy

Joe

Christopher

and *Martin*

But not Sherman.

"Come on, Ernie," Mr. Mineo said. "Let's go look for that dern fool bird."

The pickup truck splashed through the puddles of the narrow road along the lake, past the bait shop, toward

Meadville. Mr. Mineo had driven up and down this road three times since yesterday, searching the cornfields and peach orchards. He had turned onto the far end of Main Street, past the dirt driveway that led to the cluster of ramshackle houses, past the Ropers' farm, and into town. He had driven past the barbershop and the post office and the bank and Luther's Chinese Takeout. He had even gone up past the Waffle House on Highway 14.

But he had not found Sherman.

He hadn't told Ernie yet, but his aggravation was turning to worry.

CHAPTER TWENTY-TWO

Stella Feels Sorry for Herself

Stella watched as Levi and C.J. and Jiggs headed in one direction and Mutt in the other.

She definitely smelled a rat. But she was hot and hungry and wanted to go home.

By the time she and Gerald got back to Waxhaw Lane, the sun was starting to disappear behind the shiny white steeple of Rocky Creek Baptist Church. They went up to the garage roof to look for the pigeon, but he wasn't there.

So Stella went home to feel sorry for herself.

She sat in the empty doghouse in her front yard. The doghouse had been empty when Stella's family moved in, way back when she was a baby. She had asked and asked and asked if she could have a dog to live in the doghouse, but her parents always rolled their eyes and flapped their hands and then finally told her to stop asking.

When she and Gerald were little, they used to pretend they were puppies living in the doghouse. They ate pretend dog food and scratched pretend fleas and barked at the neighbor's cat when he sauntered across the yard.

Stella had given up any smidgen of hope that she would ever have a dog. But maybe if she couldn't have a dog, she could have a pigeon.

She hugged her knees and sighed.

Why did Levi have to mess everything up?

And what about Mutt Raynard?

Mutt Raynard was crazy.

There was no telling what *he* was up to.

She sat in the empty doghouse until dark and listened to her mother hollering for her from the front stoop. When she finally went inside, she had to go right to her room and say her prayers.

She sat by the open window, feeling sorry for herself and whispering into the night.

She sells seashells by the seashore.

She sells seashells by the seashore.

She sells seashells by the seashore.

The words drifted through the screen and floated across the street and hovered under the streetlights, dancing with the moths. Then they swirled up into the starry sky, where a one-legged pigeon flew above the road on the outskirts of town.

CHAPTER TWENTY-THREE

Little Brown Dog

Ethel stared up at the water stain on the ceiling of the bedroom. She had told Amos about a hundred times to get up there on the roof and fix that leak.

Amos snored beside her. The chirp of crickets drifted through the open window. The sweet scent of the honeysuckle that clung to the side of the screened porch swirled around the bedroom and mingled with the crisp, starched smell of the gingham curtains.

Ethel tiptoed over to the window and peered out into the yard, looking for the one-legged pigeon and the little brown dog.

That afternoon, while hanging the sheets on the clothesline, she had realized how much she was looking forward to seeing them.

She waited by the window, hoping they would come.

Amos snored and Ethel waited.

Amos snored and Ethel waited.

Suddenly, the silhouette of the pigeon appeared against the moonlit sky.

It swooped in circles around the top of the barn and landed on the weathervane.

Then it hopped onto the roof and disappeared through the opening under the eaves.

Ethel squinted into the darkness, searching the yard.

She waited and waited.

Amos snored.

The crickets chirped.

The gingham curtains blew gently in the breeze.

Ethel's heart sank. Where was the little brown dog?

The clock over the mantel in the dining room ticked away the minutes.

Ethel's disappointment began to grow.

Then, just as she was about to give up and go back to bed, the dog appeared at the edge of the weed-filled lot next door and trotted toward the barn. He wriggled under the fence around the old pigsty and through the open door of the barn.

Ethel held her breath, hoping the dog wouldn't bark and wake Amos up.

From the dark shadows of the barn came one little yip.

Two little yips.

Three little yips.

Then silence.

Amos stirred in the bed, grumbling and snorting, but he didn't wake up.

Ethel smiled.

She knew the dog was eating ground beef and gravy from the pie tin beneath the ladder to the hayloft.

And the one-legged pigeon was sleeping peacefully in the deserted barn-owl nest in the rafters.

CHAPTER TWENTY-FOUR

Wormy Lives Here

That night, Levi spray-painted WORMY LIVES HERE on the wooden fence beside Gerald's driveway.

Crooked red letters with paint running down and ending with drops on the sidewalk.

Gerald was sure it was Levi who had done it.

Who else would do such a thing?

Nobody.

Gerald's mother had gone out the next morning and painted over it, but the words still showed through, pale pink on the white fence.

WORMY LIVES HERE

Gerald stayed inside all morning eating ham and pickle sandwiches.

He ate three of them.

He could see Stella up on the garage roof. He heard her call him, but he didn't go out.

She came to the door three times and his mother told her he was sick. Gerald knew that Stella wouldn't believe that.

He peeked out of the kitchen window. Stella was sitting on the concrete bench under the hickory-nut tree.

Gerald heaved a sigh.

Stella was very stubborn. She would sit there for a long time.

He finished the last bite of his ham and pickle sandwich and went outside.

When Stella asked him what was wrong, he told her about the pink letters on the fence.

WORMY LIVES HERE

Stella stomped around to the other side of the fence, trampling the ivy and scaring Gerald's gray-faced dog under the porch. She picked up a hickory nut and hurled it at the fence. Then she stomped back into the yard and plopped down on the bench.

"Levi's so mean," she said. "We've got to find that pigeon before he does, okay?"

Gerald wanted to say, *No.*

He wanted to say, *I don't want anything to do with Levi and his scabby-kneed, germ-infested friends.*

But instead he said, "Okay."

He said it very quietly.

But Stella heard it.

And the next thing Gerald knew, he was following Stella up the side of Waxhaw Lane toward town.

CHAPTER TWENTY-FIVE

Edsel's Hunk of Junk

Luther hung a sign on the door of the restaurant.

GONE FISHING

Then he tossed his fishing rod into the back of Edsel's white delivery van and climbed into the front seat.

Edsel turned the key.

Whirrrrrrr clunk clunk

Edsel looked at Luther.

Luther looked at Edsel.

Edsel turned the key again.

Whirrrrrrr clunk clunk

Edsel banged his fist on the steering wheel and said a cuss word. Then he flopped his head back against the seat, pulled his baseball cap over his face, and muttered, "I hate this hunk of junk."

His neck grew redder by the minute.

Luther muttered, "Dang it."

Edsel cracked his knuckles, threw his cap onto the floor of the truck, and said another cuss word.

He turned the key one more time.

Whirrrrrrr clunk clunk

Two red lights on the dashboard blinked on.

Edsel let out a big groaning sigh. "I can't deal with this right now," he said.

While Luther and Edsel sat in angry silence in the van, Stella and Gerald ran by.

A short time later, Levi and C.J. and Jiggs rode their skateboards up the sidewalk on the other side of the street.

"Let's go eat," Edsel said.

Luther took his fishing rod out of the back of the van, and he and Edsel went inside the restaurant to eat pork lo mein. While they sat on the barstools at the chipped formica counter, Mutt Raynard loped by, whistling.

Edsel mumbled something about those crazy Raynards.

When a little brown dog trotted by, Luther tossed a piece of pork out onto the sidewalk. The dog gobbled it up, then hurried off toward the alley.

And while Luther and Edsel were sitting glumly at the counter in the restaurant, a one-legged pigeon hopped through the open back doors of Edsel's white delivery van and pecked happily at the scraps of wilting cabbage spilling through the holes of a cardboard box.

CHAPTER TWENTY-SIX

Gerald Snaps and Mutt Snoops

Stella and Gerald walked.

And walked.

And walked.

They walked up one side of Main Street and down the other.

Twice.

They walked up and down the alleys behind the shops, looking in Dumpsters and under parked cars.

Stella was feeling discouraged. "Are you even *looking*?" she snapped at Gerald.

"For the millionth time, Stella, *yes*!" he snapped back.

Stella was surprised.

Gerald never snapped.

They were heading back up Main Street when a familiar voice called from across the street.

"Hey, Wormy!"

Stella clenched her fists and glared over at Levi on the other side of the street. "Shut up!" she hollered.

"Okay, Mrs. Wormy," Levi called.

C.J. and Jiggs roared with delight.

"Just ignore them," she said to Gerald, tossing her curls out of her eyes with a flip of her chin. "Let's go back to your house."

So Stella and Gerald headed back toward Waxhaw Lane, with Levi and C.J. and Jiggs trotting along behind them, chanting "Mr. and Mrs. Wormy" and laughing up a storm.

As they walked, Stella scanned the trees and telephone wires overhead, hoping to see the one-legged pigeon. Every now and then she glared over her shoulder at Levi and C.J. and Jiggs. "Just ignore them," she whispered to Gerald, who seemed to droop lower and lower until Stella thought he might sink right down through the sidewalk.

Just as they rounded the corner onto Waxhaw Lane, Stella stopped dead in her tracks.

Mutt Raynard was doing something sneaky.

Tiptoeing along the sidewalk in front of Gerald's house.

Peering over the top of the fence.

Craning his neck to look onto the garage roof.

"Hey!" Stella yelled.

Mutt didn't jump like she'd hoped he would.

He didn't blush and look wide-eyed like she'd hoped he would.

He turned a cool gaze her way.

Stella raced toward Gerald's house.

Levi and C.J. and Jiggs raced toward Gerald's house.

Gerald trudged stoop-shouldered and heavy-footed toward his house.

They all gathered in the driveway beside the fence with the pale pink words.

Wormy Lives Here

Stella jammed her fists into her waist and glared at Mutt. "What're you doing snooping around here?"

"Who says I'm snooping?" He tossed a piece of gravel from hand to hand.

"I do."

"So?"

"So you're not allowed here."

"Says who?"

Stella looked at Gerald.

Gerald looked at his sneakers.

Levi stepped in front of Stella and put his face up close to hers. "You're not the boss of the world, Mrs. Wormy."

Stella pushed him aside and stomped over to Mutt. "You're looking for that pigeon."

Mutt kept that cool-as-a-cucumber look and said, "What pigeon?"

"That one-legged pigeon."

Mutt glanced at Levi. "There ain't no such thing as a one-legged pigeon."

Stella jabbed both thumbs toward her chest. "That pigeon is *mine*. You keep your crazy ole hands off of him and get out of Gerald's driveway." Then she tossed her head, chin in the air, and marched up the driveway toward the garage, calling over her shoulder, "Come on, Gerald."

CHAPTER TWENTY-SEVEN

Gone Fishing

When Luther and Edsel finished their pork lo mein, Edsel said, "Let's go take a look at that hunk of junk."

They went outside and Edsel opened the hood of the white delivery van. They peered down at the engine.

Luther checked the oil.

Edsel wiggled the spark plugs.

Luther examined the fan belt.

Edsel fiddled with the duct tape on the radiator. "Hmmm," he said.

Luther took his baseball cap off, scratched his head, and put his cap back on.

Edsel fished a greasy wrench out from under the front seat of the truck and tightened some bolts. He tapped the end of the wrench on a few things under the hood.

Tap

Tap

Tap

He banged the end of the wrench on a few things under the hood.

Bang

Bang

Bang

"Give her a try," he told Luther.

Luther climbed into the driver's seat and turned the key. The engine whirred and clanked . . .

. . . and then started.

Dark gray smoke puffed out of the tailpipe.

"Give her some gas!" Edsel called from under the hood.

Luther revved the engine. Rumbles and rattles echoed up Main Street. Puffs of smoke floated over the awning of the restaurant.

Edsel let out a whoop. "Let's go!" he hollered.

So Luther ran to get his fishing rod and tossed it into the back of the van. He slammed the doors and climbed into the front next to Edsel.

The white delivery van rumbled up Main Street toward the lake, with smoke pouring out of the tailpipe and a one-legged pigeon nestled contentedly inside.

CHAPTER TWENTY-EIGHT

The Boy Who Cried Wolf

Mutt jogged along the side of the road toward home, studying the cloudless sky, the rooftops of the houses, the tops of the dogwood trees. If Stella or Levi caught that pigeon, he would never be able to prove that he had been telling the truth.

A one-legged pigeon *had* landed on his head. He *wasn't* lying.

Maybe he should go to his spot at the lake in case the pigeon came back.

Or maybe he should go farther up the road past the bait shop.

Grasshoppers sprang out of the dry weeds as Mutt hurried by, his sneakers slapping on the pavement. The sun burned down on the asphalt road, leaving little bubbles of gooey melted tar here and there.

When he got to the Ropers' small brick house, he slowed to a walk. His T-shirt was damp with sweat. His hair stuck to the back of his neck.

Maybe he wouldn't go to his fishing spot after all. He studied the sky, searching.

Hoping.

But he didn't see the one-legged pigeon.

Just as he was nearing the long dirt driveway that led to his family's cluster of houses, a white delivery van drove by, clanking and rattling and leaving puffs of dark gray smoke hovering in the still summer air behind it.

Luther and Edsel.

Mutt kicked a rock on the edge of the road, sending it tumbling into the weeds.

Luther and Edsel fished all the time and lately they had been going to Mutt's favorite spot.

Mutt hated that.

One time he dragged a big rotting log across the dirt road that led to his spot, but Edsel had just driven his van around it.

Maybe he would go tell them he knew a better spot, way over on the other side of the lake.

***

When Mutt got home, his mother was mad as fire.

"Where have you been?" she hollered.

"Fishing," Mutt said.

His mother thumped him on the side of the head and said, "Don't lie to me."

Mutt glanced out the window and saw all his dirty-faced cousins playing in the yard.

"Hallie Pearson seen you in town with Levi and them other troublemakers," his mother said, her fists jammed into her waist and her eyes narrowed in that mad way of hers.

"I was looking for that one-legged pigeon I told y'all about," Mutt said.

His mother flapped a dish towel at him. "Get on out yonder and help your daddy with the lawn mower like you're supposed to."

Mutt stomped out the door and clomped down the steps and brushed past his cousins on his way to the garage out back. He pretended he didn't see them hopping around the yard on one foot and flapping their arms like wings. He pretended he didn't hear them calling out "Hey,

Mutt, there's a one-legged pigeon on your head!" while they laughed and tossed gravel at him.

Mutt shook his fist at them before he went into the garage. He would show them. He was going to catch that pigeon no matter what.

CHAPTER TWENTY-NINE

Mr. Mineo Mused and Tossed Pork Rinds

Mr. Mineo sat in a canvas camp chair in front of the bait shop, eating pork rinds. Every now and then, he tossed one down to Ernie and sighed. He hadn't been feeling like himself lately.

Normally, he felt happy and content.

He had so many reasons to feel happy and content.

He lived in a nice trailer by the lake.

He owned a bait shop and earned enough money to buy groceries and pay the light bill and put gas in his pickup truck.

He had a very fat dog he loved and who loved him back.

And he had a weathered blue shed full of homing pigeons.

But now a little glimmer of sadness was starting to buzz around him like a pesky fly.

"I don't know, Ernie," he said. "I've just got a bad feeling about Sherman."

Ernie cocked his head and wagged his stubby tail.

"He's a rapscallion, no doubt about it." Mr. Mineo tossed a pork rind onto the gravel parking lot.

"I don't know . . ."

Toss.

"He's never been gone this long."

Mr. Mineo had put six Xs on the calendar on the wall in the bait shop. Sherman had been gone for six days.

Toss.

"Maybe he's scared of Amy."

Toss.

"Which he oughtta be. I know she's red-hot mad at him."

Toss.

"Which she oughtta be."

Toss.

"All them others fly off over the lake and then come back like they're supposed to, but not that dern fool Sherman." Mr. Mineo glanced up at the sky. "Heck, he's liable to be anywhere."

Toss.

Ernie gobbled the pork rind before it even hit the gravel and smacked and crunched and slobbered.

The two of them went on like that the rest of the afternoon.

Mr. Mineo tossing pork rinds and musing out loud about Sherman. Ernie being a good listener and gobbling up the pork rinds.

When Mr. Mineo tossed the last one, he stood up with a loud, heavy sigh. "Let's go let them birds out again," he said. "Maybe they can find Sherman."

So he locked the bait shop, climbed into the truck, and headed for home with Ernie sitting contentedly beside him.

CHAPTER THIRTY

Evening Settles In

As the sun sank lower in the summer sky, the streetlights along the sidewalks of Main Street flickered on.

Over on Waxhaw Lane, Stella and Gerald put the cards in the shed at the back of the garage roof.

Stella studied the branches of the oak tree overhead, hoping the pigeon would be there.

But he wasn't.

Gerald tried to make the knot of worry in his stomach go away. How much longer was Levi going to call him Wormy?

Levi and C.J. and Jiggs carried their skateboards under their arms and headed for home. Levi was determined that tomorrow he would find that pigeon.

Mutt Raynard wiped his greasy hands on his shorts

and put the lawn mower in the garage. As he headed back to the house, his cousins hopped on one leg and flapped their arms. He chased them home, grabbing at the backs of their shirts and pulling their hair and making two of them cry.

In the rusty trailer out by the lake, Mr. Mineo sat in his old plaid lounge chair in the dark with Ernie at his feet. He had let the pigeons out after dinner, and they had flown across the lake and then they had come back.

Edna
Frankie
Martha
Samson
Leslie
Taylor
Amy
Joe
Christopher
and *Martin*
But not Sherman.

On the edge of a secluded cove of the lake, Luther and Edsel packed up their fishing gear and stretched and yawned. It hadn't been a very good day for fishing. As Luther snapped the lid shut on the tackle box and Edsel folded up the lawn chairs, a one-legged pigeon hopped out of the back of the white delivery van and flew off over the trees.

And a little brown dog trotted along the road to Mr. Mineo's.

CHAPTER THIRTY-ONE

Little Brown Dog

Amos was always grumpy when he woke up from his morning nap.

Ethel could see him out in the yard, muttering.

Every now and then, he threw his arms skyward and hollered, "Why me?"

Or glared at the ground and grumbled something Ethel couldn't make out.

She poured a tall glass of sweet tea and went out to the backyard. "Here," she said, thrusting the glass toward Amos.

He took the glass and didn't even say thank you.

Ethel had to try very hard not to snap *You're welcome!* She didn't want to make Amos any grumpier. Sometimes when Amos was really grumpy, he went out to his workshop in the corner of the barn to putter. He fixed drawers that were stuck or put a new nozzle on the garden hose or started making a birdhouse that he would never finish.

And if he went to his workshop in the corner of the barn, he might see the pie tin full of food that Ethel had put there for the little brown dog. If that happened, she and Amos would argue.

Why was she encouraging that mangy mongrel to stick around? he would ask.

If that fleabag kept him up one more night, he was going to call the dogcatcher, he would warn.

And if that one-legged pigeon showed up again, they would be having pigeon stew for dinner, he would threaten.

Usually, Ethel liked a good argument. But today she just wasn't in the mood. It was too hot and her gout was bothering her again. She was going to ask Amos to come inside and help her shuck corn, but before she could get a word out, he went on a tirade about moles in the garden.

"They're tunneling right through the tomato plants," he griped.

"Why can't they go somewhere else?" he grumbled.

"And what about that dern dog of yours?" he said.

"What do you mean?" Ethel said.

"I mean, if that flea-infested mongrel is going to come snooping around here every night, why can't he at least keep moles out of the garden?"

Ethel jammed her fists into her waist. "Amos Roper," she said, "stop picking on a poor little ole dog that hasn't even got a home. If you spent half the time you spend complaining, doing something useful instead, like fixing that kitchen drain, you could . . ."

And so it went.

Amos and Ethel argued for the rest of the morning.

CHAPTER THIRTY-TWO

Harvey

There he is!" Gerald jumped up, pointing into the branches overhead. The trash can turned over and cards scattered across the roof of the garage. Some of them fluttered down into the shrubbery below.

"Dang it, Gerald," Stella whispered. "Be quiet. You're gonna scare him away."

She peered up into the branches. Sure enough, there was the pigeon. "Don't move," she mouthed silently to Gerald.

Stella held her breath. The pigeon blinked down at her and cocked his head.

Please.

Please.

Please.

Stella begged silently.

Please fly down here.

She sent her thoughts up through the branches.

And then . . .

. . . miracle of miracles.

The pigeon flew down out of the tree and landed on top of the shed at the back of the garage roof.

Stella looked at Gerald. His mouth was open, his eyes wide.

She put her finger to her lips. "Shhhhh." She tiptoed toward the shed.

One foot in front of the other.

Slowly.

Slowly.

Slowly.

When she got closer, she stopped. Her arms hung limply at her sides.

She took a breath in.

She let a breath out.

Her heart was pounding in her ears.

The pigeon hopped around on the tin roof.

Tap

Tap

Tap

Stella held her finger up toward the pigeon.

And he hopped right on!

Stella's insides swirled with excitement. She looked back at Gerald, grinning. "He likes me," she whispered.

The pigeon's one claw clung to her finger. She stroked his soft gray feathers. He pecked at her. A gentle peck. Like a pigeon kiss.

She held him gently with both hands and walked carefully back to the lawn chairs. She sat down and cradled the pigeon in her lap. He made a soft, warbley, cooing sound.

Stella could hardly believe her good luck. She had found the pigeon before Levi had!

She began to imagine all the things she would do with him.

She would make him a comfy little cage on top of the shed on the garage roof.

She would feed him popcorn and birdseed from a Dixie cup.

She would let him fly around over Meadville every day, and then he would come back and land on her shoulder and keep her company.

At night, he would sleep in a cozy little bed that she would make out of one of her father's old flannel shirts.

"His name is Harvey," she told Gerald.

Harvey was the name Stella had picked out for the dog she had wanted for so long. Harvey was a good name for a dog, she thought. And now it was a good name for a pigeon.

Stella and Gerald spent the rest of the day playing with Harvey.

They drew a pigeon town on the garage roof with colored chalk. They drew houses and watched Harvey hop from house to house.

They added roads with stop signs and a lake with boats. They drew a church and a birdseed store and a Chinese takeout restaurant.

They sang "Home on the Range," and Harvey hopped around the pigeon town like he was dancing.

They tried to teach him to carry a card and put it into a coffee can, but he never quite got the hang of it.

It was the most fun Stella had had all summer.

It might have been the most fun Stella had had in her whole life.

And then, while Harvey was hop, hop, hopping from the chalk lake to the chalk church, someone called out from the street below:

"Yoo-hoo! Wormy!"

CHAPTER THIRTY-THREE

Mr. and Mrs. Wormy

Levi!

Gerald clutched his stomach.

His heart felt like it was going to bust right through his T-shirt.

"Dang," Stella said. "He better not come up here." She tiptoed to the edge of the roof and peered out toward the road.

"Do you see him?" Gerald asked.

Stella motioned for him to be quiet.

"Mr. and Mrs. Wormy!" Levi called from the sidewalk out front.

Gerald watched Harvey hopping to the chalk birdseed store, where Stella had put some crumbled saltine crackers. His knees felt trembly. He sat on the hot tar roof of the garage, in the middle of the chalk lake, and wished he hadn't eaten so much cereal that morning.

"Mr. and Mrs. Wormy!" Levi's singsong voice was closer now.

"Let's put Harvey in the shed," Stella whispered.

Gerald nodded.

Stella scooped the pigeon up and placed him gently inside the shed. Just as she was shutting the door, Levi's head appeared at the edge of the roof.

Gerald tried his best to look like someone who didn't care about Levi.

"You're not supposed to be up here!" Stella hollered, racing over to the ladder.

"I'm not *on* the roof, Mrs. Wormy."

Stella stomped on Levi's fingers and he grabbed at her leg, but she jumped back just in time.

Gerald sometimes enjoyed it when Stella and Levi hit and kicked at each other like that. He admired the way Stella never cried and how she thought of so many ways to fight.

Levi glared over at Gerald, his eyes scanning the chalk pigeon town. "Hey," he said. "What's that?"

Gerald wished he could go over there and stomp on Levi's fingers like Stella had. He wished he could call Levi names and push and shove him and not care one little bit if Levi called him Wormy.

But he couldn't.

All he could do was sit there forlornly and wish his mother would come out and make Levi go home.

"What's that?" Levi asked again, pointing at the chalk houses and roads and church and lake.

"None of your business," Stella said.

"Have y'all got that pigeon?" Levi glanced around the garage roof.

Gerald felt his face turn red. He kept his eyes on the pigeon lake and his mouth shut tight. He could *not* lie. He had tried many times but just never could manage to do it.

He would *think* a lie.

He would open his mouth to *say* a lie.

But he never could actually *do* it.

He always told the truth, even when he didn't want to.

He sat silently now, waiting for Stella to say something. She jammed her fists into her waist, stomped her foot, and hollered at Levi, "Go away!"

"Okay, Mrs. Wormy," Levi said. "But if I catch that pigeon, he's *mine*."

Levi disappeared down the ladder. When Gerald heard his sneakers crunching on the gravel driveway and then slapping on the sidewalk as he ran up Waxhaw Lane, he stood up and brushed blue chalk from the seat of his shorts.

"Why didn't you just tell him the truth?" he said.

Stella rolled her eyes. "'Cause I know Levi," she said. "He'll be sneaking around here with his nasty ole friends." She glanced back at the shed. "I have an idea."

Gerald felt a groan rise up from inside his worried stomach.

"We'll build a cage for Harvey on top of the shed," Stella said. "Then Levi and them can see plain as day that Harvey belongs to me. *And*," she added, "they can't come up here and take him."

A whole slew of thoughts swirled around in Gerald's head.

How were they going to build a cage?

What would they feed the pigeon?

If they let him out of the cage, would he fly away?

If he flew away, would he come back?

What if Levi caught him?

On and on and on went Gerald's thoughts.

Meanwhile, Stella had gone back to the shed to get Harvey. But when she opened the door, the one-legged pigeon hopped out and flew away.

CHAPTER THIRTY-FOUR

The Boy Who Cried Wolf

Mutt packed up his tackle box and fishing gear. Maybe his special fishing spot wasn't so special anymore. He'd been here all afternoon and hadn't even gotten a nibble.

He was just turning to head up the path to the road when he saw something out of the corner of his eye.

Something flying. Circling over the sandy patch along the edge of the lake.

Mutt stood still, barely taking a breath.

And then . . .

. . . the one-legged pigeon landed on his head.

Mutt's heart raced. He lifted his arms very, very slowly.

A little higher and a little higher and a little higher.

Slowly, slowly, slowly.

Holding his breath, he placed both hands on the pigeon. Then he lifted the bird off his head and held him in front of his face. The pigeon stared at him with his round orange eyes. The iridescent green feathers on his neck sparkled in the late-afternoon sun.

"Hey, feller," Mutt whispered.

The pigeon made a cooing sound.

Suddenly, Mutt remembered something.

"Shoot!" He stomped his foot, making the pigeon squirm a little in his hands.

He had forgotten to bring a box. He had planned on putting the pigeon in a box so he could take him home and show all the other Raynards that he had *not* been lying.

A one-legged pigeon *had* landed on his head.

He put the pigeon under his T-shirt. It was warm and soft against his stomach.

Then he hurried up the middle of the road toward home.

CHAPTER THIRTY-FIVE

Pigeon Pie

Mr. Mineo watched the pigeons swoop out of the weathered blue shed, circle a few times, and then soar out over the lake.

Edna
Frankie
Martha
Samson
Leslie
Taylor
Amy
Joe
Christopher
and *Martin*
But not Sherman.

Instead of getting to work cleaning the shed, Mr. Mineo sat on the wooden bench at the edge of the water and talked to Ernie. "Here's what must have happened," he said, scratching the fat dog's head. Ernie let out a deep doggie sigh and rested his chin on Mr. Mineo's shoe.

"Sherman must have taken off away from the others in that rapscallion way of his." He swatted at the gnats circling around Ernie's head. "You know, that rebel thing he does just to aggravate me."

Mr. Mineo gazed out over the lake. The pigeons were just tiny dots in the distance now.

"Then," he continued, "I bet he flew toward Meadville and got confused."

Ernie snored.

"Yep." Mr. Mineo nodded. "I'd bet dollars to doughnuts that's what happened." He took off his old straw hat and waved it in the air, muttering, "Dadgum gnats."

He scanned the trees along the side of the lake. "That dern fool bird better not get tangled up with them crazy Raynards over yonder." Mr. Mineo jerked his head toward the road, chuckling. "He's liable to find hisself in the middle of a pigeon pie."

He stood up, placed his straw hat back on his bald head, and made his way up the path to the shed, while Ernie still snored by the bench. He swept out the shed and hosed off the perches and refilled the water bowls. Then he took a coffee can full of seed down to the edge of the lake and shook it, calling, "Come and get it!"

Before long, the pigeons appeared in the distance. As they got closer, Mr. Mineo continued shaking the can until the pigeons circled a few times, landed on top of the chicken-wire cage on the side of the shed, and hopped inside, one by one.

Edna
Frankie
Martha
Samson
Leslie
Taylor
Amy
Joe
Christopher
and *Martin*
But not Sherman.

CHAPTER THIRTY-SIX

The Story Continues

That night, a light rain fell.

Weighing down the Queen Anne's lace along the road.

Making little ripples out across the lake.

Pattering softly onto the sidewalks of Meadville.

In the rusty trailer, Mr. Mineo slept soundly in his old plaid lounge chair, his whiskery chin resting against his chest and Ernie curled up on the floor at his feet.

Over on Waxhaw Lane, Stella whispered out of her bedroom window.

Harvey

Harvey

Harvey

Across the street, Gerald tossed and turned in his

bed. A fan whirred back and forth on the dresser, blowing the thin white curtains out like ghosts in the night.

On Main Street, Luther snored loudly in his tiny room over the restaurant.

Up in Rock Hill, Edsel tossed a wrench into his tool kit, turned off the porch light, and went back in the house, grumbling about his hunk of junk.

At the end of the long dirt driveway on the outskirts of town, Mutt sat by his bedroom window, peering through the dark toward the garage behind Emmaline Raynard's house. He hoped like anything that pigeon wouldn't get out of the box stashed behind the tires and tools and flowerpots. He had poked plenty of holes in the box with garden shears. He had made a soft bed inside it with some cotton stuffing he had pulled out of a hole in the ratty sofa on the front porch. Tomorrow he would prove to everyone once and for all that he was not crying wolf.

And out by the Ropers' barn, the little brown dog sat in the rain beside the old pig trough and howled.

CHAPTER THIRTY-SEVEN

Little Brown Dog

I'm telling you," Ethel said, "there's something wrong with that dog." She buttered a piece of toast and tossed it onto the plate in front of Amos.

"You can say that again," Amos said, spreading home-made blackberry jam on the toast.

"Seriously," Ethel said, "that poor little thing sat out there in the rain all night long."

"Waiting for you to bring him a pot roast dinner," Amos grumbled. He sopped egg yolk off the rim of his plate with a piece of toast and popped it into his mouth.

Ethel stomped over to the refrigerator and put the jam away. Then she whirled around and glared at Amos. "Why you wanna go and be so grumpy every minute of the day?" she said, flapping a dish towel in his direction.

Amos made a gravelly *hmmph* noise.

Ethel yanked his plate away. She dropped it into the sink full of sudsy water and looked out the window to the backyard.

She had gone out to the barn first thing that morning to look for the little dog. The pie tin beneath the ladder to the hayloft was still full of oatmeal and two pieces of bacon.

She had searched the rafters up by the eaves to see if that one-legged pigeon was there, but the rafters and the old barn-owl nest were empty. She was pretty sure the pigeon hadn't come the night before. She was pretty sure that was why the dog had been howling in the rain.

Now she was worried and Amos was being so grumpy.

She untied her apron and hung it on the hook behind the back door. "I'm going to go look for him," she said.

She grabbed her purse off the little table in the hall and went outside, letting the screen door slam shut behind her. She climbed into their blue-and-white station wagon and started the engine with a roar. But just as she was starting down the driveway toward the road, Amos burst out of the front door and hurried down the porch steps, hollering, "Gosh darn it, Ethel, wait for me."

CHAPTER THIRTY-EIGHT

Levi's Plan

Levi and C.J. and Jiggs sat on the curb, throwing dirt clods at the UPS truck until the driver came out of the hardware store and hollered at them.

"Where do you think that pigeon is?" C.J. said.

Levi shrugged. "Could be anywhere."

"I bet he's gonna go back to Gerald's garage," Jiggs said.

The three of them sat in silence for a while, tossing pebbles into the storm drain. Old Mrs. Banner clomped by and gave them a dirty look. Tollie Sanborn peered through the front window of the barbershop at them, shaking his head.

Suddenly, Levi jumped up and snapped his fingers. "I have a plan!"

CHAPTER THIRTY-NINE

Stella Mopes and Gerald Makes a Dough Ball

Stella sat on the edge of the roof, letting her legs dangle over the side. She clunked her heels against the garage.

Clunk

Clunk

Clunk

She lifted her shoulders and dropped them with a big heaving sigh.

Gerald came out of the back door carrying two sandwiches. His gray-faced dog loped along behind him. From the bottom of the ladder, he called up, "Want one?" and held a sandwich up for Stella to see.

She shook her head. She wasn't hungry.

"It's bologna and mustard," Gerald said.

She shook her head again.

Gerald clutched the sandwiches in one hand and climbed the ladder to join her on the roof. He sat beside her, dangling his chubby legs over the edge. He placed one sandwich on his knee and began to tear the other one into pieces.

He popped the pieces into his mouth one by one, making smacking noises as he chewed.

Stella heaved another sigh. She watched Gerald out of the corner of her eye. He rolled a piece of bread into a ball of dough.

Around and around between his palms.

Stella glanced back at the chalk pigeon town. The houses and the roads. The church and the birdseed store. She searched the tree branches overhead. She sighed again.

Gerald squished the dough ball between his fingers, making it flat, like a tiny pancake. Then he rolled and rolled it between his palms again. It was starting to turn a little gray.

"I don't know if we should go look for Harvey or wait here in case he comes back," Stella said.

Gerald shrugged.

Stella clunked her heels against the side of the garage again.

Clunk

Clunk

Clunk

That dough ball was starting to irritate her.

"Maybe one of us should go look for him and one of us should stay here," she said.

Gerald popped the gray dough ball into his mouth. Then he started tearing the other sandwich into pieces. "But what if Levi and them show up?" he said, squeezing his eyebrows together in that worried way of his.

"So?"

"So, um, I don't know, I'm just—"

"Don't be such a baby, Gerald." Stella wanted to snatch those sandwich pieces away from him. She sat on her hands and stared down at Gerald's dog, panting below them. She stood up and studied the trees overhead again.

If only Harvey would come back. This time she would keep him in the shed until she and Gerald could make a cage for him. Levi was *not* going to get him.

"Let's go look for him," she called to Gerald.

Stella was just starting toward the ladder when she heard a familiar noise.

The rumble of skateboards on the sidewalk.

She motioned for Gerald to be quiet.

The rumble stopped.

Voices drifted up to the roof from the sidewalk below.

"I'm sure it was him. How many ONE-LEGGED PIGEONS do you think there are around here?"

"Levi!" Stella whispered to Gerald.

"So he was heading out toward the LAKE?"

"Jiggs," Stella whispered. She cocked her head, straining to hear.

"Not so loud," Levi said. "Stella's liable to be around here somewhere."

Stella lifted her eyebrows and looked at Gerald, wide-eyed.

"Anyway," Levi continued, "I'm pretty sure I saw him headed toward the LAKE. You know, on that road to the BAIT SHOP."

Stella nodded at Gerald and whispered, "They're talking about Harvey."

"Let's get our bikes and go over that way and LOOK FOR HIM."

"C.J.," Gerald whispered.

"Okay," Levi said. "If we find him out there by the BAIT SHOP, we can catch him and he'll be OURS."

Then the rumble of skateboards grew fainter and fainter.

"He might be trying to trick us," Stella said.

Gerald kept quiet, hoping Stella didn't have one of her good ideas.

"But then, maybe Harvey *is* out there by the lake," Stella went on. She dashed to the ladder. "Come on!" she hollered. "Let's go!"

CHAPTER FORTY

The Boy Who Cried Wolf

Mutt hurried to the garage behind Emmaline Raynard's house. The door had come off its hinges long ago and lay on the ground, covered with kudzu. Mutt stepped inside the garage and squinted into the darkness. He stepped over the tires and tools and flowerpots. The cardboard box was still there, safe and sound. He lifted a flap and peered inside. The pigeon was nestled in the sofa-stuffing nest, blinking up at him. Mutt let out a sigh of relief.

Just then, the low, steady purr of a cat drifted through the dark, damp garage.

Mutt looked down.

One of Emmaline's cats was rubbing his head against his legs.

Purr

Purr

Purr

The pigeon rustled slightly inside the box.

"Dern it," Mutt said. "Go away, Skipper."

But Skipper stayed. The fur on the back of his neck stood up. The tip of his tail twitched.

Mutt hurried to close the flap of the box, but he tripped over the dented bumper of Jackson Raynard's old Chevy, and fell backward against a rusty bicycle with two flat tires. The box tipped over and the pigeon flew out and fluttered wildly around the garage. Mutt scrambled to grab Skipper, who crouched menacingly by the door, but the cat hissed and swatted at him with bared claws.

Mutt's heart pounded as he watched the pigeon swoop around the garage, bumping into shelves overflowing with car parts and empty soda bottles and landing from time to time on a ladder or sacks of potting soil or a crate of old roller skates and mildewed baseball mitts.

All the while, Skipper watched from the doorway, tail a-twitching.

CHAPTER FORTY-ONE

Gerald Wishes He Hadn't Eaten That Dough Ball

Gerald followed Stella down the ladder, one heavy foot after the other.

She was jabbering away about getting their bikes and heading out toward the lake and how they would find Harvey before Levi did.

Stella always made everything sound so easy.

But it never was.

He made a list in his head of the reasons he didn't want to go out to the lake:

- It was kind of a long way out there.
- Part of the road was uphill, and it was hotter than usual today.
- What if they ran into Levi and his nasty friends?

- And what if they *did* find Harvey? How were they supposed to catch him?
- And what would they do with him if they *did* catch him?

So many problems that Stella hadn't thought of.

Stella wasn't nearly as good at thinking of problems as Gerald was.

Now she was running home to get her bike.

Gerald was supposed to get his bike and meet her out front. He wished he hadn't eaten that dough ball. He clutched his stomach and plodded over to where his bike was propped against the fence along the driveway.

He couldn't stop himself from looking at those pale pink words.

Wormy Lives Here

The dough ball felt like a cannonball in his stomach.

He pushed his bike up the driveway toward the road, one heavy step at a time.

Clomp

Clomp

Clomp

Stella was waiting out front, sitting on her dented bike,

her curls standing up like springs on top of her head. She grinned at him.

"Let's go!" she hollered as she pedaled up Waxhaw Lane.

Gerald glanced over his shoulder at the garage behind his house.

How he longed to go back up there and sit in the lawn chair and play cards all day.

Instead, he climbed onto his bike and pedaled slowly after Stella.

CHAPTER FORTY-TWO

Little Brown Dog

Ethel ignored the car honking behind her. She was not going to speed up. She was looking for the little brown dog, scanning the roadsides and fields and yards.

Every once in a while, she asked Amos, "See anything?"

He would utter a grumbly "No."

She stuck her arm out the window and motioned for the car behind her to go around. The car roared by, sending up a swirl of dust.

Ethel made a *hmmph* sound.

Amos mumbled a cuss word.

"Keep your eye out for that pigeon, too," Ethel said. "If we see the pigeon, that dog is liable to be nearby."

They drove through neighborhoods and up dirt lanes

and down bumpy gravel roads. They drove behind gas stations and circled parking lots and wove through trailer parks.

But they didn't see the little brown dog.

Or the one-legged pigeon.

Amos kept asking Ethel what she was going to do if she found the dog, and Ethel kept saying, "Don't worry about it." Actually, she wasn't really sure *what* she would do if she found the dog. She just wanted to make sure he was okay.

"Let's go drive around the lake," she said, turning down the road to Mr. Mineo's.

When she got to the run-down bait shop, she pulled into the parking lot.

"Go see if it's open," she said to Amos. "Maybe Mr. Mineo has seen something."

"Aw, that old guy ain't never here," Amos said. "Anybody that wants to fish is better off digging their own dang worms."

But he got out and shuffled across the parking lot to the bait shop.

He tried the door.

Locked.

He knocked on the window.

Nothing.

He climbed back into the car, grumbling something about wanting to go home.

But Ethel wanted to find the little brown dog.

CHAPTER FORTY-THREE

Edsel's Hunk of Junk (Again)

On the road to Mr. Mineo's, Luther and Edsel heard a familiar noise coming from under the hood of Edsel's white delivery van.

Sort of a *whirrrrrr-clunk-clunk* noise.

Then swirls of dark gray smoke twisted into the air like little tornadoes on each side of the hood.

"Gol-dern criminy cripes," Edsel muttered. "I'm ready to push this hunk of junk right into the lake and call it a day."

Luther didn't say anything. He knew Edsel well. When that vein on the side of his neck started pulsing like that, it was better to keep quiet.

The van putt, putt, putted to a stop.

There was a slow *sssssss*, two puffs of gray smoke, and then nothing but the still summer air.

The buzz of a fly.

Luther clearing his throat.

Edsel pounding the steering wheel.

"This gol-dern hunk of junk."

Luther and Edsel got out of the van. Edsel opened the hood. The loud squeak of metal echoed across the field of wildflowers on the other side of the road.

Smoke billowed out from under the hood.

There was a brief *tick-tick-tick* sound.

Luther and Edsel peered down at the engine.

Luther checked the oil.

Edsel wiggled the spark plugs.

Luther examined the fan belt.

Edsel fiddled with the duct tape on the radiator.

They tugged on hoses and jiggled wires and poked at stuff.

Then they stood back with their hands in their pockets and stared at the engine, frowning.

"I reckon we're gonna have to walk up to the bait shop and call for a tow," Edsel said.

"I reckon," Luther said.

Luther and Edsel looked up the road.

Waves of steamy heat hovered above the asphalt. Queen Anne's lace and wild blackberries grew on either side. The rain the night before had left little puddles scattered here and there. Kudzu snaked its way up a speed limit sign with a couple of rusty bullet holes in it. Up ahead was a neglected peach orchard, the trees dried and brown, the ground littered with rotten peaches. The narrow road ahead of them wound lazily through fields of corn and soybeans.

It looked like a long walk to nowhere.

"Wanna rest up first?" Edsel said.

"Sure."

Edsel stretched out on the seat of the van, his head on the armrest and his legs dangling out of the door.

Luther opened the back doors, pushed aside the fishing rods and tackle boxes, and flopped down on a dirty canvas tarp with his baseball cap over his face.

Before long, deep steady snores echoed across the Carolina countryside.

CHAPTER FORTY-FOUR

Eight Xs and a Toothpick

Mr. Mineo put another X on the calendar.

Eight.

He went out front and sat on the bench beside the WORMS FOR SALE sign. Ernie curled up at his feet.

"Maybe I should just give up," Mr. Mineo said.

"Maybe that dern fool bird has found hisself a new home."

He sighed.

"Wouldn't surprise me a bit."

He rubbed Ernie's back with the toe of his shoe.

"He always was a little too cocky."

He glanced up at the sky.

"Hoppin' around that shed like he owned the place."

He chuckled.

"He don't even know he's only got one leg."

Mr. Mineo took a toothpick out of the pocket of his shirt and chewed on the end of it.

"Well, good riddance is what I say."

He shifted the toothpick to the other side of his mouth.

"And good luck to whoever's got him now."

He studied the treetops on the other side of the road.

"Right, Ernie?"

Ernie stirred slightly in his sleep. Mr. Mineo sat in front of the bait shop all morning, chewing on the tooth-pick and watching the sky.

Finally, he said, "Dagnabbit, Ernie, let's go look one more time."

CHAPTER FORTY-FIVE

The Boy Who Cried Wolf

Mutt whistled and held his hand out toward the pigeon fluttering around the garage.

"Come here, fella," he whispered.

But the pigeon would not come. He flew up to the rafters at the top of the garage and blinked down at him.

Skipper crouched in the doorway.

Mutt turned to the cat and hollered, "Get on out of here!"

But Skipper stayed.

Then Lola, Emmaline's fluffy white cat, came sauntering over from the yard.

And then Coco, the skinny one.

And Nellie, the orange one.

Skipper and Lola and Coco and Nellie.

Lined up side by side in the doorway of the garage, tails twitching, eyes gleaming. The silence in the garage was thick and heavy.

Mutt looked from the cats to the pigeon.

From the pigeon to the cats.

Silence.

Silence.

Still, still, silence.

Then Mutt lunged toward the cats, flapping his arms and hollering, "Shoo! Go! Get!"

Which made the pigeon flutter wildly around the top of the garage.

Which made the cats leap on tires and boxes and flowerpots and ladders, swatting the air with their sharp claws and getting closer and closer to the one-legged pigeon.

CHAPTER FORTY-SIX

Levi and C.J. and Jiggs Whoop It Up

Levi and C.J. and Jiggs roared with laughter as Stella and Gerald disappeared around the corner of Waxhaw Lane.

"I *told* you she'd fall for it," Levi said, beaming at C.J. and Jiggs. "She's a ding-dong doodlebrain."

They slapped each other's backs and high-fived and whooped it up until finally Levi said, "Now we've got to get up there on Gerald's garage and wait for that pigeon."

The three of them dashed across the street to Gerald's house. They tiptoed up the driveway and along the shrubbery to the ladder.

Levi shot a quick look over his shoulder to the back door of Gerald's house, then whispered, "Come on."

CHAPTER FORTY-SEVEN

Stella Wouldn't Slow Down

Stella pedaled and pedaled and pedaled.

Every now and then she glanced behind her at Gerald.

His face was red. His hair was damp with sweat. He huffed and puffed and hollered, "Slow down!"

But Stella wouldn't slow down.

She was going to find that pigeon before Levi did.

No matter what.

She pedaled past the hardware store and the church and on out toward the outskirts of town. She passed the Ropers' small brick house with the big wooden barn.

She passed the dirt driveway that led to the cluster of ramshackle houses where the Raynards lived.

Then she turned down the road that led to the lake.

The road to Mr. Mineo's.

As she pedaled, she scanned the trees and rooftops and telephone wires, searching for the pigeon. But she didn't see him.

She studied the road ahead, looking for Levi and C.J. and Jiggs. But she didn't see them. She was starting to worry that maybe Levi *had* tricked her.

CHAPTER FORTY-EIGHT

The Story Continues

Mr. Mineo drove his pickup truck on the side roads of Meadville. His fat dog, Ernie, sat beside him with his head stuck out the window, panting in the summer breeze. Every once in a while, Mr. Mineo got out of the truck and rattled a can of birdseed, calling, "Come and get it!"

Meanwhile, Stella and Gerald pedaled their bikes along the narrow road toward the bait shop. Stella looked very determined, searching the trees and rooftops along the way.

Gerald looked very hot and tired. His face grew redder by the minute as he tried his best to keep up with Stella.

Ethel Roper drove her blue-and-white station wagon around the lake, searching for the little brown dog and the pigeon. Amos slouched beside her, grumbling.

Luther and Edsel slept in the white delivery van on the side of the road.

Over on Waxhaw Lane, Gerald's mother yelled at Levi and C.J. and Jiggs to get off her property before she called the police, sending them scampering down the ladder from the garage roof and racing home.

In Emmaline Raynard's garage, Mutt flapped his arms and hollered at the cats, while the one-legged pigeon swooped and fluttered above them.

And the little brown dog trotted up the dirt driveway toward the cluster of ramshackle houses.

CHAPTER FORTY-NINE

The Boy Who Cried Wolf

Mutt's heart raced.

The cats jumped onto sacks of fertilizer and climbed over car parts and leaped onto rusty paint cans and tractor tires and milk crates.

Mutt tried to grab them, but they hissed and yowled and darted away from him. He tried to grab the pigeon, but it flapped and fluttered and swooped from one side of the garage to the other.

And then suddenly . . .

. . . a little brown dog burst into the garage, barking and carrying on like crazy, chasing the cats around and around until they scurried outside.

Then everything got calm and quiet.

The dog sat in the corner of the garage and stared up at the pigeon, his tail swishing back and forth on the cool cement floor. The cats sat out in the yard in the shade of a scrawny dogwood tree, grooming themselves and looking annoyed. The pigeon nestled in the rafters of the garage and cooed softly down at the dog.

Mutt's heart settled down, and he let out a sigh of relief.

But just when it seemed like the commotion was over, all those Raynard kids whose names started with the letter *B* came running from around the side of Emmaline's house. They made such a racket that the dog darted out of the garage, raced across the yard, and scampered off into the woods. Then the pigeon swooped down from the rafters and soared out of the open door, disappearing over the top of the house.

"Gol-dern it!" Mutt hollered, shaking his fists at the kids. "Look what y'all done!" He pointed at the sky over Emmaline's house. "That was the pigeon I told y'all about."

"What pigeon?" Byron said.

"The one that landed on my head." Mutt tapped the top of his head.

"I didn't see no pigeon," Brassy said.

"Me neither," Becka said.

"He's only got one leg." Mutt held a finger in Becka's face and she slapped at it.

Then one of the kids said, "You're such a liar, Mutt."

"Yeah, you're such a liar, Mutt," another one said.

Then they all started hopping around the yard on one leg, chanting, "Mutt is a liar. Mutt is a liar." Mutt chased them and yanked their hair and slapped their legs and punched their arms until they ran off toward home.

Mutt glared up at the sky. Now he was more determined than ever to catch that pigeon.

CHAPTER FIFTY

By the Side of the Road

I give up," Mr. Mineo said to Ernie. "That dern fool bird is gone, and I say good riddance to him."

He studied the cloudless sky. "If he gets hungry enough, he'll come home."

He scanned the tops of the trees on the side of the road. "Aw, heck with him, right?" He glanced over at Ernie, curled up on the seat beside him.

"Let's go get some lunch." He turned the pickup truck in the direction of the bait shop.

Just as he rounded a curve in the road, he spied something on the side of the road ahead.

A white delivery van.

"That's *Edsel's* van," he said.

He turned the truck onto the grass by the roadside

and stopped. Just as he was getting out, a car pulled in behind him.

A blue-and-white station wagon.

Amos Roper got out of the passenger side and waved to Mr. Mineo. "Got trouble?" he said.

Mr. Mineo shook his head. "Not me." He nodded toward Edsel's van.

The hood was up.

Edsel's feet were hanging out of the side door.

Luther's feet were hanging out of the back doors.

And snores echoed across the Carolina countryside.

CHAPTER FIFTY-ONE

Levi Has Another Plan

Levi and C.J. and Jiggs sat glumly on the curb in front of the barbershop, tossing pebbles into the storm drain and listening to them hit the water below the grate.

Ploink

Ploink

Ploink

"What do y'all want to do now?" C.J. said.

Levi shrugged. He glanced across the street at Luther's Chinese Takeout. A sign hung on the door:

GONE FISHING

The three of them sat in silence.

Suddenly, Levi sat up straight and whispered, "Don't move."

C.J. and Jiggs didn't move.

"That pigeon is over yonder," Levi whispered.

Sure enough, the one-legged pigeon hopped around in front of the restaurant, pecking at the sidewalk.

"What do we do now?" Jiggs whispered.

Levi thought.

Then he told C.J. and Jiggs his plan.

Two of them would stay here and keep an eye on the pigeon, while one of them went to the convenience store up the street to buy something to lure him. Crackers or chips or popcorn.

Then they would tiptoe across the street, and one of them would make a trail of crumbs up the sidewalk while the other two waited in the alley.

The pigeon would hop up the sidewalk, eating the crumbs.

And then, when he got near the alley . . .

. . . *bingo!*

They would nab him.

CHAPTER FIFTY-TWO

The Boy Who Cried Wolf

Mutt was steaming mad. As he made his way up the side of the road, he kicked at rocks.

Hard.

Each time he kicked a rock, he called out one of his cousins' names that started with the letter *B*.

He was so busy being mad and kicking rocks that he didn't notice Stella and Gerald riding toward him until he nearly ran smack into them.

Stella stopped. "What are *you* doing out here?" She narrowed her eyes at him.

"I *live* out here," he said. "What are *you* doing out here?"

Stella glanced at Gerald, who stood there looking tired and red-faced. "We're just riding our bikes." She gave Gerald a poke. "Right, Gerald?"

"Right," he said, shifting from foot to foot in that nervous way of his.

"Bye." Mutt waved at them and continued up the road toward town.

"Wait!" Stella called after him. "Have you seen that one-legged pigeon?"

"Yes." Mutt called over his shoulder as he continued up the road.

Stella jumped off her bike and ran after him. "Really?"

"Yes." Mutt kept walking, looking straight ahead, wanting Stella to go away.

"You have not." Stella stomped her foot. "You're such a liar."

Mutt stopped. His face turned red. He clenched his fists and kicked at the dirt on the side of the road, sending up swirls of dust. He yanked at weeds and threw rocks and stomped on his baseball cap.

Stella and Gerald watched with wide eyes and gaping mouths.

When Mutt was through kicking and clenching and throwing and yanking and stomping, he picked his baseball cap up, dusted it off, and looked coolly at Stella. "I *did* see that pigeon," he said. "He landed on top of my head yesterday at the lake. I put him under my shirt and took him home. I made a nest for him in a cardboard box and kept him in Emmaline's garage all night. This morning, I went to check on him and he got out of the box and Emmaline's cats tried to catch him. Then a stray dog showed up and chased the cats away, but all my crazy cousins made a commotion and scared the dog and the pigeon away."

Then Mutt put his baseball cap back on and continued up the road, leaving Stella and Gerald standing in silence.

CHAPTER FIFTY-THREE

When Levi's Plan Didn't Work

Levi and C.J. and Jiggs stood slump-shouldered on the sidewalk in front of Luther's Chinese Takeout, watching the one-legged pigeon swoop through the summer sky toward the outskirts of town.

Levi's plan hadn't worked.

They had made a trail of crumbs on the sidewalk and hidden in the alley and jumped out to grab the pigeon. But C.J. had tripped and fallen, Jiggs had made too much noise, and Levi hadn't been quick enough.

After they argued for a minute or two about whose fault it was, they ran home to get their bikes. Then they raced up Main Street, past the bank and the post office, toward the fields and farms outside of town, looking for the pigeon.

While Levi and C.J. and Jiggs raced *out* of town, Mutt Raynard stomped angrily up the middle of the road *toward* town. He kicked rocks and mumbled under his breath about being sick and tired of everyone calling him a liar.

Suddenly, he caught sight of the pigeon flying in the opposite direction toward the lake. So he quit all of his kicking and mumbling, turned around, and raced back down the road after him.

CHAPTER FIFTY-FOUR

Stella Doesn't Like What She Hears

On the road to Mr. Mineo's, Stella and Gerald pedaled their bikes toward the bait shop. Stella searched the treetops, and Gerald huffed and puffed and hollered, "Wait up!"

When she rounded a curve and saw a blue-and-white station wagon, a pickup truck, and a white delivery van on the side of the road ahead, she slowed down.

Luther and Edsel sat in the weeds at the edge of the woods, yawning and looking sleepy-eyed.

Mr. Mineo leaned over the engine of the van and twisted wrenches and jiggled wires. His fat dog, Ernie, scratched at fleas and snapped at flies.

Amos Roper sat behind the wheel of the van and turned the key. The engine whirred and clanked and rattled.

Ethel Roper stood beside the station wagon and searched up and down the road, looking worried.

Stella jumped off her bike. "Have y'all seen a pigeon?"

Mr. Mineo straightened up so fast he hit his head on the hood of the van.

Bang.

Gerald stopped his bike beside Stella, panting. His freckled arms were pink with sunburn.

Mr. Mineo adjusted his straw hat and wiped his greasy hands on his trousers. "I'm looking for a pigeon, too," he said.

"So are me and Amos." Ethel glanced into the treetops. "And a dog," she added. "A little brown dog."

Stella felt a tiny knot in her stomach. "The pigeon I'm looking for only has one leg," she said.

"That's Sherman!" Mr. Mineo nudged his dog scratching and snapping beside him. "How about that, Ernie?" He turned back to Stella. "Sherman is one of my homing pigeons."

Sherman?

Stella's heart sank. "His name is Harvey," she said in a soft, pitiful voice. "Right, Gerald?" The tiny knot in her stomach was growing into a very large knot.

Gerald wiped sweat off the back of his neck and mumbled, "I guess."

Stella clutched her stomach and looked down at the ground. She almost always knew what to do, but now she didn't.

She wanted to stomp her feet and cry like a baby.

She wanted to punch Gerald.

She wanted to tell Mr. Mineo he was wrong. That pigeon was *not* Sherman. That pigeon was Harvey, and he belonged to *her*.

But before she could do anything, Mutt Raynard came trotting up the road toward them.

Not far behind him, Levi and C.J. and Jiggs raced full steam ahead on their bikes hollering at each other about which one of them had messed up Levi's plan.

Then right in the middle of all that trotting and racing and hollering, the one-legged pigeon appeared overhead. He circled the deserted peach orchard a few times and then swooped down and landed on the telephone wires along the side of the road.

And the little brown dog darted out of the orchard, barking up a storm.

CHAPTER FIFTY-FIVE

Everyone Watches Sherman

Mr. Mineo's heavy heart lifted when he saw his one-legged pigeon with the shiny green neck and two black stripes on his wings.

He whistled to the bird.

Sherman cocked his head and cooed.

The little brown dog stopped barking.

Mr. Mineo whistled again and held his finger up. Sherman blinked down at him with his round orange eyes, but he stayed put.

"Dern fool bird," Mr. Mineo mumbled. He shuffled over to his pickup truck and got the can of birdseed. He rattled the can while everyone watched.

Stella and Gerald.

Amos and Ethel Roper.

Luther and Edsel.

Mutt Raynard.

Levi and C.J. and Jiggs.

Ernie and the little brown dog.

But Sherman would not come down.

"I'm so aggravated," Mr. Mineo muttered. He rattled the can again.

But Sherman would not come down.

Mr. Mineo scratched his chin. Then he snapped his fingers. "I have an idea!"

Everyone looked at Mr. Mineo, waiting to hear his idea.

"I'll go home and get Amy. Sherman will listen to *her.*"

Then he explained to everyone about Amy and that temper of hers and how she was liable to be mad as all get-out but could make Sherman go back home where he belonged.

So he called for Ernie, and the two of them took off in the pickup truck toward the rusty trailer beside the lake.

CHAPTER FIFTY-SIX

Little Brown Dog

Ethel Roper reached into the pocket of her skirt and took out a limp slice of orange cheese wrapped in a paper towel. She held it out toward the little brown dog.

The dog looked from the pigeon to the cheese.

From the cheese to the pigeon.

From the pigeon to the cheese.

Ethel handed the cheese to Stella. "You give it to him," she said.

Stella took the cheese from Ethel and held it out in the palm of her hand.

The dog took one more glance at the pigeon and then trotted over to Stella. He ate the cheese in one big gulp and licked Stella's hand.

He licked and licked and licked.

Then he sat in front of her, wagging his tail.

Stella grinned at Ethel. "He likes me."

Ethel smiled at Stella and nodded.

As the minutes ticked by, Stella stopped worrying so much about the one-legged pigeon hopping up and down the telephone wires above her. She sat on the side of the road and hugged the little brown dog.

CHAPTER FIFTY-SEVEN

Waiting

While everyone waited for Mr. Mineo to return with Amy, Sherman fluttered from the telephone wires to the trees. From the trees to the top of a rotting fence post beside the orchard. From the fence post back to the telephone wires.

Stella sat beside the little brown dog, stroking his fur and scratching behind his ears. The knot in her stomach was getting smaller and smaller.

Ethel Roper smiled at them and wished she had another piece of cheese.

Amos Roper fiddled with the engine of the delivery van while Luther and Edsel dozed in the grass beside the road.

Levi and C.J. and Jiggs hurled rocks into the woods, sending loud *thwacks* echoing through the trees.

Gerald watched them, wishing he could hurl rocks, too, and hoping those scabby-kneed boys wouldn't call him Wormy.

Mutt Raynard thought about going home, but he knew his dirty-faced cousins would be there, hopping and flapping and calling him a liar. So he hurled a few rocks into the woods and wished Sherman would fly down and land on his head.

But Sherman didn't move.

CHAPTER FIFTY-EIGHT

Mr. Mineo's Spirits Are Lifted

Okay, now listen, Amy," Mr. Mineo said to the pigeon in the wicker basket on the seat beside him. "I know you're fire-spittin' mad at that dern fool Sherman." He patted the top of the basket. "And lord knows you've got every right to be."

Ernie sniffed at the basket and Amy fluttered a little.

"You know how stubborn he is," Mr. Mineo continued.

Amy cooed. The truck bounced along the driveway from the trailer to the road.

"If he's gonna listen to anyone, it's you. Right, Ernie?" Mr. Mineo nodded at his fat dog sitting on the other side of the basket.

As they turned onto the road and passed the bait shop,

Mr. Mineo urged Amy to watch her temper and just persuade Sherman to follow her back to the weathered blue shed behind the trailer.

Amy blinked up at him through the holes in the basket.

As they drove along, the warm summer air swirled around inside the pickup truck, blowing Ernie's ears back and lifting Mr. Mineo's spirits.

CHAPTER FIFTY-NINE

Amy to the Rescue

With each wag of the brown dog's tail, the knot in Stella's stomach had grown smaller and smaller until it had disappeared completely.

When Mr. Mineo returned, Stella joined the others as they gathered around. The little brown dog trotted along behind her.

Mr. Mineo got out of the truck, carrying a small wicker basket with a cooing pigeon inside. He set the basket on the ground and opened the lid. A white pigeon with black speckles soared into the air.

The kids let out a whoop.

Luther and Edsel slapped their knees and hollered, "Go get him, Amy!" and "Thatta girl, Amy!"

Amos Roper leaned against the delivery van, looking

grumpy, while Ethel smiled up at the speckled pigeon circling the sky above them.

The little brown dog let out one bark and sat in the road next to Stella, wagging his tail and watching the pigeons.

Mr. Mineo waved his straw hat in the air. "Come on, you dern fool bird."

Amy circled and circled while Sherman stayed on the telephone wire, head bobbing and feathers ruffling.

Everyone waited.

Sherman hopped up and down the wire a few times.

Amy circled and circled.

Everyone waited and waited.

Suddenly, Sherman soared into the sky, circling above them with Amy.

The air was filled with whoops and hollers and claps and barks.

Then the two pigeons took off, side by side, toward the lake.

CHAPTER SIXTY

On the Road to Mr. Mineo's

Come on!" Mr. Mineo hollered as he scrambled into his truck.

Luther and Edsel climbed in the front with Ernie squeezed between them, while Mutt jumped into the back.

Amos and Ethel hurried to their blue-and-white station wagon. Ethel opened the back door and the little brown dog jumped right in.

Stella and the others hopped on their bikes.

Then they all took off down the road to Mr. Mineo's.

CHAPTER SIXTY-ONE

The Weathered Blue Shed

When he got to the bait shop, Mr. Mineo turned down the driveway that led to his rusty trailer by the lake. The Ropers' blue-and-white station wagon pulled in after him. Not far behind the Ropers, Stella and the others raced up on their bikes.

Mr. Mineo hurried down the path to the weathered blue shed, motioning for the others to follow. He stepped inside and pointed at the pigeons, calling their names, one by one:

Edna

Frankie

Martha

Samson

Leslie

Taylor

Joe

Christopher

and *Martin*

But not Amy and Sherman.

Mr. Mineo's whiskery face drooped as he stepped out of the shed, shaking his head and telling the others that Amy and Sherman were not there.

A deep, heavy silence fell over them all.

But then . . .

. . . the little brown dog raced down to the lake, barking up a storm.

The others hurried after him.

When they got to the water's edge, Mr. Mineo pointed at the sky.

Amy and Sherman were soaring over the lake, swooping and gliding with the late-afternoon sun sparkling across the still surface of the water. Then Sherman began to fly lower . . .

. . . and lower . . .

. . . and lower . . .

. . . until he fluttered down and landed right on top of Mutt Raynard's head.

At first, Mutt's mouth dropped open in surprise. Then

he beamed at everyone while Amy circled above them. But suddenly, the little brown dog let out one sharp bark and Sherman soared back into the sky.

Mr. Mineo waved his straw hat, and the others waved their arms and whistled and called to the pigeons. They all watched as Amy and Sherman flew closer and closer, then skimmed the tops of the trees beside the lake and finally landed on the roof of the weathered blue shed.

Everyone raced back up to the shed just in time to see Amy give Sherman one sharp peck on the head before they both hopped through the bars of the window and disappeared inside.

CHAPTER SIXTY-TWO

Everyone Tells Their Stories

Everyone cheered when Amy and Sherman hopped into the shed.

Then they sat on the rickety porch of Mr. Mineo's trailer and told their stories.

Mr. Mineo told the others about his brother, Carl, who had gone to live in a nursing home and had given him the pigeons. The pigeons lived in the shed behind his trailer and twice a day they flew out across the lake and then came back. Except for Sherman, who had been missing for eight days and had worried him half to death.

Ethel Roper told them how the pigeon had been flying into their barn at night and the little brown dog chased after him and barked half the night, making Amos grumpy.

Mutt Raynard told them how the pigeon had landed on his head when he was fishing and how no one believed him. He explained how he had wanted to catch the pigeon to prove he had been telling the truth. But when he finally caught him, Emmaline's cats had chased him around the garage and the dog had chased the cats and his wild cousins had scared them both away.

Levi told them how the pigeon had swooped into the carport when he and C.J. and Jiggs were flipping bottle caps into the middle of an old tire. Then he had tried to catch the pigeon before Stella did because she didn't know diddly-squat about pigeons.

Luther and Edsel scratched their heads and yawned.

Gerald just sat there looking worried.

With the little brown dog snuggled next to her, Stella told the others how the pigeon had landed on the garage roof and she and Gerald had drawn a pigeon town with colored chalk. She told them she had named him Harvey and she had wanted to keep him because she wanted a pet.

After everyone told their stories, Mr. Mineo invited them to go up to the bait shop for a soda.

And so they did.

CHAPTER SIXTY-THREE

Where the Story Ends

As night settled over Meadville, the crickets chirped and eighteen-wheelers rumbled out on Highway 14. Streetlights cast a soft amber glow on the sidewalks of Main Street. The pecan trees that lined the street rustled softly in the gentle summer breeze, like a whisper.

The sound of snoring drifted out of the window of the tiny room over Luther's Chinese Takeout. Fishing gear rested against the wall by the door, ready for another day out at the lake with Edsel as soon as the delivery van was fixed.

Over on Waxhaw Lane, in the big white house with the blue-striped awnings, Gerald Baxter smiled in his sleep as he dreamed about giving Levi the Knuckle of Death.

Across the street, Stella sat by the window of her

bedroom in the green house with muddy shoes on the porch and whispered into the night:

Harvey

Harvey

Harvey

Earlier that evening, she had begged and begged her parents to let her keep the little brown dog. When Ethel Roper told them what a good dog he was and how he needed a home, they had finally said yes.

Stella named him Harvey, and now he was fast asleep in the doghouse in the front yard.

On the outskirts of town, Ethel Roper sat on the side of the bed and gazed out at the moonlit yard, thinking about how nice it was that the dog had found a little girl to love him. Behind her, Amos slept peacefully under the crisp white sheet.

Just beyond the Ropers' small brick house, in one of the ramshackle houses at the end of the long dirt driveway, Mutt Raynard lay in his bed and grinned up at the cracked plaster ceiling. He *had* been telling the truth about the one-legged pigeon, and tomorrow he would take his wild cousins to see for themselves.

Out in the rusty trailer by the lake, Mr. Mineo snored

softly in his old plaid lounge chair. His fat dog, Ernie, was curled up on the rug at his feet, dreaming about pork rinds.

And behind the trailer in the weathered blue shed, Sherman nestled on a perch beside Amy, cooing softly, while a full Carolina moon shone down on the road to Mr. Mineo's.